Henry G. Cole

Confessions of an American Opium Eater:

From Bondage to Freedom

Henry G. Cole

Confessions of an American Opium Eater:
From Bondage to Freedom

ISBN/EAN: 9783337274955

Printed in Europe, USA, Canada, Australia, Japan

Cover: Foto ©Raphael Reischuk / pixelio.de

More available books at **www.hansebooks.com**

CONFESSIONS

OF AN

AMERICAN OPIUM EATER

FROM BONDAGE TO FREEDOM

Timely advised, the coming evil shun:
Better not do the deed than weep it done.
— *Prior.*

BOSTON
JAMES H. EARLE
178 Washington Street
1895

CONTENTS.

CONTENTS.
(CONTINUED.)

APPENDIX.

ILLUSTRATIONS.

By ARTHUR GEARFIELD LEARNED of Chelsea, Mass.

Without creed, but not without faith.

PREFACE.

It becomes the author to say that the pages published in this volume have had their birth in poverty, have been reared in adversity, and have been compiled and sent forth in the hope that attention will be drawn to the pernicious Opium habit, and they will illustrate the manner in which the author found deliverance from the Opium bondage.

These experiences have no relation whatever to the "mind healers' art," the Christian Science doctrine, or to any sect or creed. The motive for their publication has been actuated by no selfish ambition or pecuniary gain.

The author is painfully conscious that they contain glaring imperfections when contrasted with the writings of men of letters, who have portrayed the delights and sufferings by the Opium habit, but who, unfortunately, have been deprived of the privilege of singing the song of redemption in this world. The potency of Coleridge's wail, "When I am dead," is almost sufficient to deter him from sending these "Confessions" forth during his sojourn in the land of the living. If the reader discovers the author's reasoning conflicting with his own religious training or thoughts, let him bear in mind that in no sense is this work written other than that for which expression has already been made.

Since these experiences were purchased by great and unmitigated suffering, to be an unknown benefactor to humanity would be far more in harmony with his feelings than to be the possessor of all the halo that clusters around the brow of the world's great saviours of ·mankind.

The illustrations in this work are intended to represent bona-fide experiences, and are not put in for embellishment alone.

THE AUTHOR.

Brookline, Mass., March 10, 1895.

CONFESSIONS.

CHAPTER I.

PRELIMINARY.

"After my death, I earnestly entreat that a full and un-qualified narrative of my wretchedness and of its guilty cause, may be made public, that at least some little good may be effected by the direful example." COLERIDGE.

"It is almost like Dives seeking for a messenger to his brethren; but tell them—tell all young men what it is, that they come not into this torment." REQUEST OF A DYING OPIUM EATER.

"The sentiment which attends the sudden revelation that ALL'S LOST! silently is gathered up into the heart; it is too deep for gestures or for words. * * * Upon seeing those awful gates closed and hung with draperies of woe, as for a death already past, I spoke not, nor started, nor groaned. One profound sigh ascended from my heart, and I was silent for days." DE QUINCY.

THE above extracts are incorporated here by the author, not that they are isolated and exaggerated expressions of the despair that wells up from the soul and finds vent in the only method man has of sending forth the warning cry to his fellow-travelers on life's highway, but rather that they are weak, and feebly express the agony and remorse of numberless perishing souls who have borne testimony in like manner to those immediately connected or associated with them in their dying moments, but which have never been given to the world; not from any feeling of pride, however, but from the fact that no scribe stood by to take down and send forth their dying protests to unborn generations "that they come not into this torment."

The Opium Eater (the cognomen by which the author will be known in these pages) will not wait, however strong may be his desire, like Coleridge, until death removes him from the living, to bear witness to that which was the cause of untold wretchedness and despair in his own life; and, more wonderful still, to that which has brought joy unspeakable and hope, freedom, and emancipation from the opium curse.

Since the days when De Quincy and Coleridge and countless others indulged in the use of opium, man's ingenuity has brought forth many inventions; and an "opium eater," so-called—one addicted to the use of opium in a crude state—is perhaps a rarer thing now than in the days of those individuals, on account of said discoveries. Both of these gentlemen's "opium eating" consisted principally in using vast quantities of laudanum—an alkaloid made from gum opium.

It would be a task for which I am unqualified, to detail the numberless poisons that today are in use, the victim of almost any one of which would be classed in the category of an "opium fiend." The fact that almost everywhere throughout our land, institutions for the cure of those addicted to some one of the many drug habits — to say nothing of those reared for alcoholic inebriates—would be in itself an ample apology for this work. These institutions are the outgrowth of a demand on the part of those who are seeking an asylum to be liberated from a bondage they are unable to emancipate themselves from.

The utter ignorance of the frightful arena into which the Opium Eater at last found himself, and the vain attempts to retrace his steps to freedom and liberty from his relentless captor, — Opium, — makes it almost imperative that the rising generation be made more familiar with the facts of this awful existence which came to him, blasting all hopes of pleasure and enjoyment in this beautiful world, by doubly destroying the temple which the Infinite Mind has created for our happiness.

Freedom after years of incarceration in a prison may be sweet to the prisoner, but time will not efface, nor the joy of liberty compensate, for the guilty act which brought about the cause of his punishment. As this narrative will show, after perfect emancipation from morphia and total abstinence from all other stimulants, and years of perfect health, — God's great gift to man, — far rather would it have been my choice to have known and thus escaped the evil, than to have purchased the knowledge of it at so fearful a price. Hence, then, these "Confessions" are for those who will heed and profit by the mistakes of the Opium Eater and others herein narrated.

Perhaps outside of intemperance from alcoholic stimulants, the most common forms of drug-taking might be found in Munn's Elixir of Opium, morphia, laudanum, and cocaine; snuff being also extensively used by other than "fallen" women.

It is, however, the intention of the writer to deal prin-

cipally with his experience in the use of morphine, hypo-
dermically injected, all other intoxicants, drugs and anæsthetics having found a culmination in this popular method
of using opium. The Opium Eater has never "eaten"
opium, except on one occasion — if holding in one's mouth
a piece of the crude drug until it had crumbled up, can in
any sense be called "eating" it. However, the experience
was of so little moment, being addicted at the time as I
was to the more powerful form of using it subcutaneously,
that it leaves only the remembrance of something not unlike crumbling and bitter spruce gum, expectorated before
any effect was produced on my already opium-filled body.

Together with the Opium Eater's personal experiences,
he has incorporated those of others which he thinks will
add weight to his own. The works on the subject are
comparatively meagre, — outside of those known to the
medical profession, — only three having come under the
writer's observation in his search in the public libraries of
Boston and elsewhere, the famous one, "The Confessions
of an English Opium Eater," by De Quincy, — which, by
the way, has without doubt been the innocent cause of
many a lost soul, — being the most prominent; "The
Opium Habit," published by Harper Brothers; and another
small book, a few extracts borrowed from which will be
found in this volume with due credit.

"Better bear the ills we know, than fly to those we
know not of," is an applicable text to the sorrow-stricken
and afflicted mortals who seek solace and comfort in the
potency of opium, under innumerable names.

Man has gathered from the ages and woven into proverbs the sign-boards that should and would guide many

lives into the sunlight of a perfect day, but for a "little learning that is a dangerous thing," that has changed these priceless jewels into airy nothings. Hence, they say a little wine and a little folly, and not too much of a time-immemorial prohibited vice, become a blessing and not a curse. And experience again demonstrates the Truth of her broken laws in those rash enough to violate them.

The world today contains untold numbers of noble men and women who, through a lack of knowledge, have become the slaves of some one of the many remedies prescribed by physicians or made enticing by the advertisers' art, to relieve them from an overworked and overtaxed system. It goes without contradiction that physicians are, strange to say,—yet not strange, either, when we recall the exacting duties of their profession,—numbered among opium's ready victims. There is no department of life, no order of society, from the highest to the lowest, that cannot muster a large roll of opium takers. I come in contact with its victims almost everywhere; and that knowledge, and thereby security and immunity from a life of bondage, the power to break from which has not yet been discovered in the realm of medical science by the student or the careful and conscientious practitioner, would in itself alone warrant these "Confessions" being placed before the world.

Had the Opium Eater come in contact in his younger days with a book that would have served as a beacon light to reveal the terrible hell that lies in the pathway of all men from the use of opium, I do not think I should now be recording "The Confessions of an American Opium Eater." If I may be pardoned for criticising so wonder-

CHAPTER II.

CONCERNING MY EARLY LIFE.

THE OPIUM EATER first saw the light on the 10th day of March, 1851, in the beautiful city of Portland, Me., situated at the head of the three hundred and sixty-five islands in Casco Bay. Of my parents I shall here say but little. And yet, one only has to look at his progenitors to find the mirror which reflects himself, to a large degree. It was one of those cases where opposite natures meet. On the one hand the loftiest, and purest, and holiest aspirations and ambitions that fill the human soul — love, virtue, purity — the Christian graces; on the other, "a hail fellow's" life, so artfully concealed that association and experience alone remove the veil that blinds the eyes of confiding love, and reveal the true character of duplicity and hypocrisy. The former picture belongs to my mother; the latter may be an overdrawn one of my father. My mother may truly be said to have had for a father a Puritan of the Puritans, and a descendant from the original colony that landed at Plymouth in 1620; and yet her spirit, like that of her noble mother, was the spirit of the Pilgrim in its loftiest, and highest, and broadest sense.

With such characteristics as I have described as belonging to my parents, the thoughtful reader will readily see that the time must come when a line of demarkation and separation must follow. And come it finally did; and the man of the world, of pleasure, and of selfishness, throws aside responsibilities the most sacred and solemn that man can enter into in this world, and left in young life a large family of children—eight sons—to the "tender mercies" of a selfish world and the care of a loving and devoted mother.

My opportunities for an education, therefore, were very limited; and, in the vernacular of the gambling world, I never lived up to the "limit." With relation to the subject of which I am treating, however, it probably would have made little or no difference, the victims of this terrible and ever-increasing passion or habit finding its votaries not in the unlearned and so-called ignorant classes, but rather are to be found among the refined and cultivated,—proving that learning is not the embodiment of all wisdom; or, as the apostle has put it, "ever learning, and never able to come to the knowledge of the truth."

The passion which largely entered into my boyhood was that which partook of the nature of games of chance. I preferred gambling for marbles to eating or sleeping. And I find mankind are only children of a larger growth in this particular. Even in the innocence of childish amusements there enters the same spirit that makes it impossible of any other result than those to be found in maturer games of gambling. The games of the youth are often so constructed that a shrewd boy can fortify himself behind the inevitable law of a sure thing, and abstaining from play on the "outside," the devices of his inventive genius enables him often to become a veritable Crœsus in marbledom.

So we graduate from one stage of the game of chance to another. From marbles to pennies, from pennies to cards, from cards to faro and the horse-track,— the latter run the year round solely in the interest of the professional gambler and the pool-box, who reap a golden harvest from the uninitiated; and last, but not least, many who do not gamble on the most solemn and sacred duty they owe to themselves and their country,—the election of public servants,—are not only beneath notice, but bring upon themselves the ridicule and contempt of their associates for maintaining opinions unsupported by "filthy lucre." And so in this matter it is as I once heard a temperance lecturer, who was on a "spree," remark in regard to people who did not do as he was then doing, "There are two classes who never drink—fools and misers. One class does not know enough; the other are too mean." In other words, if you don't gamble, you are a fool or miser. Some writer has recently said that gambling is as universal as lying.

From an incident that occurred bearing on the sentiment of religion, as I found it in the forming period of my youthful life, and which will tell more than a multiplicity of words of what is not, what should be, and what we have a right to expect from those who teach the precepts of religious life and are our examples and lights, and what we often receive, I relate the following.

I went to live at an early age with my mother's parents. A grand and noble Christian soul was my good grandmother—a veritable mother in Israel; full of good deeds, beloved and honored by all, and owned in a special manner of God. Yet her religious life manifested itself not in outward devotions. I never heard her in prayer. She

probably followed her Master's injunction, "When thou
prayest, enter into thy closet, and when thou hast shut
the door," etc., for the manifestation of such devotion was
made apparent in her every-day life.

My grandfather, however, was very religious. With
him, the words of God as contained in the Bible were the
only ones Jehovah had ever spoken or ever would speak.
His morning and evening devotional services were exacting, and consumed nearly if not quite an hour. Yet,
while he clung so tenaciously to God's Word, and read in
it that "no Scripture given by inspiration of God is of private interpretation," he invariably read from his Bible a
few verses, to be followed by copious draughts from the
marginal notes or "private interpretations" from Scott's
Commentary.

Returning home from the service of his church one
Sunday evening, he found me deeply interested in a
book—some good book, but not God's Book. He asked
as to its kind and nature, and after inspecting it, and finding no crying evil in it worthy of anything more than talk,
he concluded by asking, "Have you read the Bible today?"
to which I replied in the negative. The matter was dropped
with the injunction that on the next Sabbath evening I
should be able to answer "Yes" to a similar interrogation.

Things shape themselves peculiarly if all is haphazard
in the affairs of men, and chance happens to bring about
things very singularly, sometimes, to say the least. It
was in the winter months, and the next Sunday night, between my grandsire's leaving for and returning home from
church, a howling northeast snowstorm had commenced,
and the wind was moaning, and shrieking, and howling

around the corners of the house and outbuildings, and hurling snow and hail against the window panes, when, suddenly, I heard the stamping process as of one removing snow from the feet, and my grandfather's presence I momentarily expected. Forewarned is forearmed, and I always made the most of any opportunity to absent myself from the family altar.

But now, suddenly, like a flash, there entered my mind the command of the previous Sabbath evening. He had not mentioned it since—I had not thought of it. It was too late now to perform the task. Before he was through the door, however, cat-like, I was springing up the stairs, and in a jiffy I was snug in bed.

The first thing I remember hearing him say to his good wife was—

"Where's that boy?"

"Gone to bed," replied my saintly grandmother.

And then at the foot of the chamber stairs I heard his voice calling to me to come down. But I was asleep (to him). And, wicked soul, I allowed him to drag his more than three-score-years-and-ten, yet lithe frame, to my chamber door, where, in a voice not gentle and meek, I was ordered out of bed to attend the evening prayers, as he said. Yet the first words he uttered, when I had descended below, were, "Have you read the Bible today?" showing that another motive alone actuated him.

I made him no answer. Two spirits of like nature and character stood face to face; one firm in his seventy odd years of religious zeal; the other, a youthful "heretic," but a trifle over two thirds of one score in years. He was determined; I was resolute.

"ANSWER ME, YOU SIR, OR LEAVE THIS HOUSE!"—(*page 15.*)

Again he put the question. I did not reply to it.

"Answer me, you sir," he shouted, thoroughly aroused, "or leave this house;" and suiting the action to his words he opened the door, and into the pitiless night and blinding, howling, swirling snowstorm, I went forth as commanded without uttering a word.

Our nearest neighbors were not professors of religion— that is, they did not have a prayer service an hour long, like my good grandparent,—but they were kind-hearted, good people, like all countryfolk; the man was a little profane, sometimes, more from habit and indifference than any real wickedness, but his wife was one of the noblest of Eve's daughters. She was full of good deeds, ministered to the sick and dying, and, somehow, was so loving and charitable in her theological reasoning, as to believe that there was goodness in every one, and realizing that while she knew little, the Infinite knew much, and that in some way happiness and salvation would come to all. Of course, to my grandparent this was little short of blasphemous, and he never wearied speculating how so good a woman could be so "deluded."

I intended seeking shelter here. But in the country people retire at an early hour, and now it was late, and the house was dark, and perhaps it was best I should not disturb them. I tried my grandfather's barn; but that, too, was barred against me. Some distance away, however, there was another one, and I knew I could get in that, because in the big doors there was a small one that always could be opened; and thither through the blinding storm I made my way, and in a few moments I stood within its sheltering precincts. And a singular reception I received.

All the cattle with one accord arose from their restful positions, and their clanking chains sent a weird and terrible sensation through my trembling soul as I stood for a moment in hesitancy before making my ascent to the mow above; and even the barnyard fowls that, unfortunately for their comfort, had gathered on the rungs of the ladder and barred my passage to the mow above, were not disposed to be courteous at all; and in my endeavor to pass on and up, some of them fell off with a dull thud. I do not remember of thinking of God. I know I did of the traditional ghosts. But I felt no fear. I burrowed into the mow of hay, and soon fell into sound and peaceful slumber.

In the morning I was aroused by voices below. They belonged to the owner of the barn and his son. My voice, out of the depths of the mow, gave them a start, as I called their name; but an explanation of my plight brought anything but a favorable comment upon the author of my discomfort.

Soon after, I passed along the road, intending to go to the city, to my home. My grandfather was clearing away the snow from his store steps. He hailed me, as I passed, and the "my son," was strangely in contrast with the "you sir" of the night before, as he asked me to continue the work he had begun, as my grandmother desired his presence elsewhere. The changed and pleasant tone and softened manner was also in harmony with my own feelings. It had been a wretched and fearful night for him, not so much on my account, but from the night-long anxiety of my good grandmother as to my whereabouts; the innocent in this case — as in most others—suffering for the

more humble sisters, in honest and constant employment.
I saw little of my father. How he lived then was, as
it ever has been, an enigma. He said on one occasion,
when I asked him for the secret, "That the world owed
him a living." But for what act or deed he did not state.
He has, however, apparently been more successful in collecting his debt from the world than the world has been
successful in collecting financial obligations from him.

When he occupied the room it was for sleep. There
was no picturesque scenery without—the high walls of
large mercantile establishments shutting out the horizon
almost from view in one direction, while lodging and board-
ing houses—long since given way to substantial business
structures — filled up the remaining circle formed by
them. Being so high up we could see little of terra firma.
But those back yards were a great rendezvous for cats —
Tabby and Thomas, too. They held high carnival in
those haunts. And an incident occurred one night, in
those early city experiences, that brings to me a sense of
humor even when I am saddest.

The noise was something diabolical, such as Boston
cats seem specially gifted in making. I heard the usual
methods adopted by timid people of "shooing" them off,
such as "s-c-a-t," and throwing some light articles in the
direction from which the unearthly yells arose. But they
failed to reach the case. Finally, my father rose rather
deliberately, with an expression I did not catch. It
was not profanity; for from my earliest recollection I
have yet to hear him swear. He once remarked to me in
this connection, "I was a peculiar rumseller; no man was
ever allowed to profane the name of Jesus Christ in my

place" (a place, by the way, historical in the annals of the
Maine law, nearly fifty years ago, when he fought it and
Neal Dow, as he said, to a constitutional finish, and having
won the victory, abandoned the soul-destroying traffic, and
declared it by placarding his saloon with the announcement "that the Maine law had not effected the change,
but a higher sense of duty which he owed to God and his
fellow-man, had alone brought about the change "). He
selected some weighty object, and raising the window, he
hesitated a moment as for a more accurate direction of
the sound, then he shied the missile forth. There seemed
a painful silence between the "letting go " and the "bringing up " of that missile, and above the high notes of Thomas below there came a sound as of an avalanche of broken
glass. He had successfully accomplished his mission, and
without comment was soon in peaceful repose, while that
which had brought tranquility to him seemed to have had
a diverse operation on the neighborhood, as the exchanged
speculations with one another manifested.

But in the new world, the big city, — alone, wandering
here and there at the concert saloons, theaters, everything
to attract,— I soon forgot home, and was swallowed up in
its frivolities. It must have been in the winter months,
for along the principal streets its saloons were placarded
with the announcement of turkey raffles ; and perhaps a
large cock turkey did duty as a decoy, and enticed the unwary and simple among men in to take a " chance." They
were veritable gambling dens. Men gathered about the
table, not unlike a "prop" table, and threw dice presuma-
bly for this symbol of New England's Thanksgiving festiv-
ities. After some unfortunate had won, the gamekeeper

would hand down a couple of dollars, more or less, and then the same process would be repeated for "another" turkey at the same rates; the inevitable result being that the commissions exacted each time would soon result in the flow of the greater part of the money into the coffers of the banker, and a crowd and the same bird complacently did service for another evening.

Then the "free and easy" concert saloons, with banjo and piano music, and for other attractions once clever men and women on the mimic stage, now fallen and debauched, eking out an existence by a mere pittance given them, and subsisting on the stimulants furnished by reckless youth and abandoned life, and exhibiting altogether a most painful spectacle. Shooting galleries, bowling alleys, and all these diversified scenes captured and allured in the evening, after a day of toil.

It was a "broad road" crowded with travelers, and the wonder is that any escape and find the "narrow" and the better way.

CHAPTER III.

MY FIRST EXPERIMENT WITH OPIUM.

CITY LIFE soon makes a transformation in the country youth, and my case was no exception. I left Boston in a few months after my advent, but soon returned, and having prospered somewhat in my occupation, I sought no more the healthy location of an attic, but occupied fashionable apartments on lower floors with my brother and his roommate, I having passed the stages where my rusticity of appearance ceased to attract.

The object lessons that are continually being enacted before the very eyes of mankind do not seem to act as leaven. Life may go out at your very side from intemperance and other sins, but the ranks are constantly recruited, and no diminution is apparent in the ever-marching hosts to blighted lives and hopeless misery and despair in this present existence. I was marching on with this indifferent host, careless and ignorant of its end.

Associating, too, with one perfectly familiar with the pathway I was treading, and having had a wholesale experience himself, I fail to remember any warning note (undoubtedly it would not have been heeded) to save me from the pit I must inevitably fall into. We will pass over these scenes, common in the life of many youth — sons and daughters alike,— and bring ourselves in closer relation with the object of these pages—the "Confessions" themselves. Before I make this rapid stride, let me fill up the gap of years by stating that I had now become familiar with the scenes characteristic with "fast" life, — the gambling house, the drinking palace, the racetrack, and the brothel and its infamous and degrading spectacle. Page upon page of incidents might be written of sorrowful scenes witnessed in these fleeting years; but in those days of profligacy I was living out in spirit the letter of Holy Writ, wherein it is written, "Let us eat, drink, and be merry, for tomorrow we die," and was hardened in the belief that consciousness is swallowed up in a death that ends all. The abandoned wrecks of humanity everywhere to be seen, and that fill our almshouses and insane asylums, are living witnesses of this sentiment and of nature's folly. The Opium Eater will, therefore, leave these years unfilled, and give their sequel in culminating events.

If the author could, in a task so disagreeable, dissociate himself from the rest of mankind and bear the burden alone, and not by hint, even, draw into the fiber of his sad story the life of another, this task would be comparatively an easy one. Doubly hard, indeed, is it when this narrative compels the lifting of the veil that death has so kindly, and, I believe, lovingly drawn over the suffering and agonizing soul whose life went out in its prime and vigor, and but for wine and the blight of opium would no doubt today be among the living, honored and blest of her sex.

If the world was lost by a woman's transgression, its salvation and redemption has, and will, come through her; and the honor and the glory that will be accorded to her by the redeemed, will be incomparable by any figure of speech, no matter how much exaggerated.

That I became a slave and a bondman to this demon
Opium, and the silken cords that held me and were woven
about me until I became a helpless and hopeless victim,
were the work of a woman—a slave to this demon herself
—I must confess.   And that to one of her sex I am,
under a Divine Providence, emancipated, and I most joyfully give the honor and the credit.   Strange to relate,—
and when I have done my tale you must confess it also,—
I never, by imprecation, word or thought, laid the charge
of my misery and sufferings to another, or felt that any
condemnation lay upon the soul of this woman for my own
lost and miserable condition.   Time and experience have
shown to me that although cultured and refined, her education had not made her acquainted with the fiend that
held the power of enchantment and death over her.   Not
always does one lead another designedly into the pit in
social and sensuous pleasures.   They rather belong to the
soul possessed by hate, and envy, and jealousy,— passions
more cruel than the grave.   I know somewhat of the
meanness and the blackness of the human heart.   I much
prefer, however, to look behind the veil, and account for
the seemingly strange happenings that come to us, than
to ascribe them to mortals who act from no motives of re-
venge, or hate, or malice.   We live and move in the same
world man has always lived in, and always will live in as
man ; subject to the same eternal laws, the same passions,
the same evil and the same good impulses.   Potiphars'
wives have been numerous in all ages of the world, are
numerous today, and will be tomorrow.   The Josephs are
as rare as they were in the days of the Pharaohs.   Had
my life and character been as fortified in virtue as was his

who was despised by his brethren and sold into Egpytian bondage, this pen would have no need of the forced employment it is now engaged in in writing these " Confessions."

On the 3d of July, 1873, I took for the first time an alkaloid of opium, known as morphia, by hypodermic injection. It was administered under conditions like this : I had been drinking somewhat to excess, and being in the company of those who were habitués to its use, I have no doubt I asked for the privilege of trying it. However, it was administered to me, it being subcutaneously injected in my forearm, a couple of inches above the wrist of the left one. I particularize this circumstance for various reasons ; the most important of which is that morphine administered below the elbow or kneejoints, or the under part of the arms or limbs, has the effect of making exceedingly sore places, and the absorption is less effective, and the result generally not so satisfactory. No doubt the student of anatomy can account for this. Morphia thus used above the joints, immediately raises a bunch not dissimilar to that of a mosquito bite, only magnified many fold. Almost instantly it shoots off into little streams upward and instantaneously the nerve centers respond like a galvanic shock to the terrible power, and wave after wave passes over the system, at times the shocks being so frequent and powerful as almost to stop the breath, and make one gasp. They become pleasant when not too precipitous. The same effect may result from an injection below these parts of the body. Of the thousands upon thousands of these hypodermic syringe marks on the Opium Eater's body above the joints, there are comparatively few below. Excruciating agony alone compelled these few exceptions. Further along in my career the pain arising from this form of using the drug would surely have made me resort to these untouched parts of the body had it been even possible without useless torment. My use, in this respect, of these portions of the body have also been the experience of others of my acquaintance, and for 'similar reasons. Why, I do not know. That it is true, physicians to the contrary, notwithstanding, is a fact.

The effect of this first "hypo" (a term that will be used largely in the remaining pages to designate "hypodermic injections") was so powerful and overwhelming that almost immediately I fell over, and desired to be let alone and sleep. I was not allowed to. For some time— I do not know how long — I was walked up and down the room. I have at this late day no vivid recollection of how the night was passed, except that a dull and heavy stupor permeated my being. And while I can look back to the scenes preceding and immediately following the taking of the drug, the remaining hours of the night remain hopelessly blank. It being the night of all nights the noisest in America,— that preceding the Fourth of July,—I had been unmindful of it so far as to noise in one of its most noisy strongholds. The next morning I felt compelled to go to my employment, being connected with a Sunday paper. The invisible forces seemed to have conspired with the visible, for no amount of persuasion could induce my foreman to grant me leave of absence, and my pride forbade me humiliating myself, and the drug seemed to still further determine me to penance and to mortification.

Concerning the ecstatic state described by De Quincy, it was anything but realized in this, the Opium Eater's first experience. I was benumbed. I was sick,—dreadfully sick. I was in the world; I did not seem of it. And yet I felt powerless to act. Mechanically I strove to do something. My spirit seemed chained within me. I managed to go through the motions of labor, but accomplished really nothing. An observer, if he did not watch too closely, would have called it work. My arms were like weights. My face was haggard, and pale beyond description. My eyes were full, dead, and almost sightless. Within I was a flaming fire, and nothing I could drink would quench it ; for nothing would stay on my stomach hardly longer than swallowing it. My mouth, and throat, and the whole membrane of the stomach seemed to have taken on a coating not unlike fur ; water would not penetrate it, nor whiskey cut it. No sooner was it taken in than it would be ejected with the force of a squirt-gun. I was keenly on the alert, above all things, that no one should discover my condition, and the excitement incidental to the day, and the isolated position I occupied in the office helped me out.

It was a long, long day, and a longer night before I got "good night." Now, while I was conscious momentarily of my doings, I could not have told what I had done five minutes previous. When I say that my memory, by constant training, enabled me to remember everything I would do from one week's end to another, even to remembering so trifling a matter as a number of lines, say two or three, scattered through the columns of a paper, I could not remember one solitary thing I did when I came to look for it in the following week. Responsibility was there, however, from the fact that I was conscious of what I was doing at the time, although not remembering it after a lapse of hours.

When finally released early Sunday morning from those long and terrible hours, I sought my couch. I have always been impressed with the thought,— and of course such a thing as recording it never entered my mind,— when looking back to that day (twenty-one years ago) that the following Monday, late in the afternoon, was the time I first awoke from my first opium stupor, some thirty-six to forty hours after retiring.

After such an experience as that, the general reader will say, How could any one ever be so foolish as to again indulge in so cursed a thing? It is passing strange; but, alas, we do! This is only a multiplication of the effect of tobacco on almost every delicate, sensitive constitution. Nature resents this invasion of a foreign foe, and fights for her purity with the only weapon at her command against her overthrow; but at last, after repeated assaults, she submits, but never wholly and unreservedly, for all along life's voyage she makes attempts to regain her first estate, — but the battle more often goes against her. A few reconquer themselves; all might.

The indulgence in both liquor and tobacco are entered into too thoughtlessly by parents. Children are brought up in constant contact with father's pipe; and parents there are who thinking it a cunning, boyish trick to see the contaminating thing in a child's mouth, have a little later in life seen him adopt the habit of tobacco using almost as naturally as ducks take to water, with a seemingly natural relish, and with none of those "upside down" and the-earth-flying-up-to-bump-you-in-the-face sensations, and the action of the limbs, too, put in motion as though two-foot obstacles were put in the pathway at every step. Man's whole nature repulses these invasions at first, in the great majority of cases ; and when they have become a forced part of his life, will not yield without a fierce battle far more aggressive and desperate than the surrender to them ; and even if mastered, the ill effects will cling, and are too often made manifest in broken health and nervous and irritable temperaments.

But how can the Opium Eater make better excuse for a further indulgence in opium than in making use of the following lines of the poet ? —

> "Vice is a monster of so frightful mien,
> As, to be hated, needs but to be seen ;
> Yet, seen too oft, familiar with her face,
> We first endure, then pity, then embrace."

As time went on, coming in daily contact with the drug and its users, and adjusting the amount taken more to my temperament, or more scientifically, so to speak, I indulged on occasions more particularly where dissipation or excessive hours of labor had exhausted nature, without giving a thought of coming slavery and bondage, and that hopeless despair was my final doom. Chloral, too, another powerful drug, played no inconsiderable part in this game of life and death. There was no more necessity for my using these drugs at that time than has my sleeping child now lying before me. No pains, no aches, no disease, no sad bereavements, no losses of friends or affections of the heart ruthlessly betrayed, — nothing but simply contact incited me to make use of them. They brought to me none of those enchanting and heavenly sensations described by De Quincey to lure me on. Morphia came to me, rather, when in other dissipations I had found the apex of enjoyment. A small quantity of this delusive fluid made of me, for the time being, a new creature, and weariness and fatigue fled, and the animal and carnal nature found expression where it otherwise would have lain dormant.

. CHAPTER IV.

AM I MY SISTER'S KEEPER? — THE PRODIGAL DAUGHTER.

WHEN Night draws her mantle over Day, the penniless outcasts and tramps, and unfortunate men unable to obtain employment, flock to the missions opened by individuals who feel an interest in the well-being of their fellow-creatures, and are endeavoring in their way to make Christ practical among the fallen. In one of these missions the Opium Eater listened, one night, to one of the prodigal sons gathered therein,— the most of them, perhaps, never having had a father in that larger sense, or a home in that sweeter and tenderer meaning of the word,—pour out the bitter cry of his life. He was past middle age. The leer of some drunken youth in front of him had much to do in bringing forth his fiery utterances. He was not a "convert." Intemperate parents, — his father having forfeited his life to the gallows through its curse,— and no guide in early life, the result had been that he had passed the majority of his years in penal institutions. And now the experiences of a bitter past had set emotions at work in his breast, and the endeavor to find more honorable means of obtaining subsistence for existence animated him. But, alas, the past walked side by side with the present, and he, at least, expressed no sentiment in harmony with the poet when he sang, —

> " Hope springs eternal in the human breast,
> Man never is, but always to be blest ;
> The soul, uneasy and confined at home,
> Rests and expatiates in a life to come,"

for his utterances bespoke one utterly crushed with despair. But the thought that brings my fellow-companion in misery and despondency to me, is the expression made use of by him that in all the years of prison life, nearly every clergyman and others who came thither to talk to the prisoners selected the theme of the Prodigal Son as the basis for their remarks, until, as he said, the Prodigal Son had been served up in so many different ways, that it was a relief to escape from the penalty of listening to them.

The reformer harps and dwells in like manner upon this spiritual outcast, — who was not so unfortunate, after all, he having found himself and his Divine origin at one and the same time. "Where is my Boy tonight?" and like beautiful emotional effusions, are all right. Little, if anything, however, is said by reform orators about one that is far more to be pitied, — the prodigal daughter. Unlike her unfortunate brother, who becomes an isolated wanderer in a far country, she may be found in numbers of from half a dozen to a score or more crowded in one house, and blocks and streets are almost entirely given up to her in almost every large city. She has become a polluted thing. No fatted calf for her is slain ; no merry-go-round, and spotless robe, and feast for her is laid. Her life is a quick and consuming fire, — thank God for that, — and a kind and forbearing Father, in his inscrutable mercy, has made provision in the future for these repentant wanderers. If the prodigal son has hardly strength to totter under the load of a degraded life, and he the stronger vessel,—where, think you, would the truly repentant prodigal daughter find strength to carry the burden of her soul except in death? O happy death! O glad release from a body polluted by sin so ghastly! How wonderful is God's mercy shown to you in His laws, my wandering, sin-sick victim of man's inhumanity! In the search for the lost one-hundredth prodigal son, the ninety-and-nine perishing prodigal daughters are left to the "tender mercy" of those who, clothed with a "little brief authority," filch them not only of their honor, but of the price of their own blood. The investigation by the New York Senate Committee, Stead's "If Christ Came to Chicago," and the Opium Eater's personal knowledge for many years, are sufficient evidence of this truth.

Am I my sister's keeper? The incident I now relate is common enough. I narrate it more from the fact that the world is full of similar incidents than from its rarity. A Christianity that had in it the Christ spirit would require no suggestion from mortal lips; its spirit would drive into uncanny regions the thought, to say nothing of the reality;— would have seen the end, and saved by prevention,— the best salvation,— a simple, loving, and innocent child.

As my grandfather's clerk in his country store, I saw, and became familiar with, scenes that now reveal the thorny path which many of his customers trod. And as I look back through the vista of forty odd years, strange

tales might I weave into fiction-truths of many of the
humble plodders who passed to and fro along the highway
with no higher thoughts associated with the daily struggle
of a life that sooner or later was to go out and be no more.
In this humble capacity, none touched me more tenderly
than a loving and beautiful little girl, with eyes so bright
and sparkling, and form so fair and lithe.   My own little
one, so beautiful, and who so fills my life, as I turn to
gaze upon her sweet and peaceful face as she lies sleeping
at my elbow, is no more beautiful and innocent than was
the one of whom I write.   Perhaps sadder, but removed
from her worse than funereal surroundings, and the joy
and the happiness of life, of which the earth is so full
to children, was hers to enjoy.   Meager indeed were her
purchases.   Her father was a drunken sot.   Her mother,
happily, had passed away, but not before the drunkard-
demon had broken her heart.   It is the old, old story.   A
fine farm drank up; tumble-down barns, no stock in them,
windows stuffed with rags, and everything abandoned by
him to the fiend that possessed him.   There were other
daughters and a son.   Refinement and education had been
his heritage, and law his profession, I think.   As like re-
produces itself, the law of reproduction had been fulfilled
in his offspring.   Hence the refining legacy to his progeny.
Yet what was vague to the then youthful mind, is clear
now.   This foul fiend, to satisfy his mania for drink, had
turned his home into a resort common in city life,— a resort unholy and lewd,—with his own flesh and blood, sacri-
ficing their souls to damn his.

    *   *   *   *   *   *   *   *   *

As the playwright draws the curtain in the prologue,

indicative of change of scene or lapse of years, so the Opium Eater will leave ten years or more behind and transfer the scene from country life and rustic habits to a great city, teeming with glare and glitter, and full of meshes for the simple and thoughtless, wherein the youth of country verdancy was being whirled hither and thither, drinking at every fountain of pleasure and momentary gratification. The drinking saloon, the gambling hell, and the brothel,— the trinity of modern damnation and disgrace,— were a part of his life.

One night, with body and brain fired by unholy passion, amid scenes by no means new or strange in profligate life, within the haunts of vice I see a face,— a beautiful face, —a face I have seen before. I look, and think, —and thought travels with lightning rapidity. I place that face. I see again before me the pure and innocent little girl of my youthful days ; the departed mother, the drunkard, the home made desolate and turned to lasciviousness and debauchery, father and son eating and drinking the blood-bought bread wrung from souls made in the image of the Creator, and fairer and more holy in their natures than His sons. The scene overpowered the blighting influence of drink and opium, and soberly I could view a picture more horrible than those drawn of the Inferno ! I had no child, no wife. No sister's loving smile had e'er been mine. The scene about me was not new, and sentimental thoughts had long since been swallowed up in the pervading one of endless death. Why should that childish face have so imprinted itself upon the tablet of my soul, that years hence, in such a place, fair and beautiful, reveal again its identity ; and, later still, to be recorded here as an incident common to the life of many a neglected, erring sister? Who led me there to behold such a sight, and see the "evil work that is done under the sun"?

While in New York, on one occasion, the Opium Eater passed through the scenes of witnessing whole blocks given over to immoral purposes, not unlike those described by the New York divine in his late crusade. In conversation with one of those " padrones " in human souls,— the "madame" of the house—she bewailed the fact of her inability to procure girls, and intimated that she would be willing to pay $15 for every girl sent to her. She did not want them familiar with New York. Of course, this is nothing new. Many an innocent country girl is swallowed up in these dens by "bogus" intelligence offices ; those custodians of protection under the law have not always used their authority in protecting innocence, but rather have acted in collusion with the procuress in entrapping friendless girls into these worse than madhouses.

The degradation of slavery pales into diminutive proportions in comparison with this vice. Men traffic in cattle, hogs, sheep, and lambs for the slaughter. But here and now, in a so-called Christian civilization, $15 is the price offered for the likeness of one who bore a Saviour to mankind, that her body may be prostituted to enrich with filthy lucre those who have become debased, and who accept the bribe and the rental of the building.

The poor among men, the outcast and prodigal of both sexes, are in need of a gospel and a heaven that has a location and a reality. The great lawgiver Moses led a vast army of mankind, century-ridden in ignorance and bondage, but he had a gospel wherein was revealed "a land flowing with milk and honey." His vast army of discontents were fed on angels' food, yet they were continually in rebellion and were an army of grumblers.

Today the same classes have preached to them a gospel of fear and eternal punishment ; a heaven, the location of which is placed "beyond the realms of time and space," and the privilege, after listening to such tidings, of reclining their weary bodies on the floor or settees, cord-wood-like, provided they have the wherewithal ; and, last but not least, beans, stale bread, coffee-slops, without milk or sugar, if a five-cent coin accompany the order. This is a true picture of a nineteenth century "gospel" mission bill of fare, as seen by the Opium Eater in his association with the outcast prodigals of the day. Surely the swine-herder of ancient times fared not less sumptuously than his prototype of today. With the needs of life-saving power as urgent now as at any time in the past, the modern mission-worker is handicapped with having no all-absorbing theme such as his ancient type possessed. He has no promised land, no angels' food, no "to your tents, O Israel;" no home-ties, no brotherhood and sister-hood, and no Fatherhood of the human race, with the all-inspiring thought of Him who "spake as never man spake," when He prayed "Thy Kingdom come, Thy will be done on earth," to inspire his utterances and beget a "a lively hope" in his hopeless hearers.

Statisticians tell us of the thousands annually marching to the grave of the drunkard ; but one rarely speaks of the nefarious business where once pure souls are sold for lustful merchandise, and where a far greater army is re-cruited from innocence and ignorance, yearly,—and for whom we can all say, without hesitancy, they enter a hell of living death, far more real and loathsome than he who, debauched and imbeciled by drink, has passed from life into. We feel a sense of relief at his demise, and trust that nothing awaits him more terrible than that from which he has happily been released.

As I close this chapter, and think of the prodigal daughters, I feel constrained to exclaim with the Preacher, when he wrote, "Wherefore, I praised the dead which are already dead, more than the living which are yet alive." And, again we say, also with him, "Yea, better is he than both they [the prodigal son and the prodigal daughter] which hath not yet been, who hath not seen the evil work that is done under the sun."

In looking upon my own loved one, I trust that I shall use that intelligence which will not hesitate to instruct the living concerning the vital issues of life, and thereby have reason to rejoice more in the living, than the "dead which are already dead."

Are you your sister's keeper? See to it, then, that innocence and purity in youth be separated from the contaminating influence of vice and depravity. "What ye would that others should do unto you, do ye even so to them." Society should have saved that lamb! I feel thankful that God's law can.

CHAPTER V.

AT THE GAMING TABLE.—THE DEATH OF MY WIFE.

MARRIAGE is ordained of God. It is the most sacred covenant entered into by mankind. The type of marriage given to humanity by the example found in our first parents, and reiterated by every prophet in the order of God, through all the ages, will ever remain. The age was not unlike our own in faithless marriage covenants, when Jesus Christ harmonized himself with those that preceded him with a divine message, when he said, "For this cause shall a man leave father and mother, and shall cleave unto his wife; and they twain shall be one flesh. Wherefore they are no more twain, but one flesh. What, therefore, God hath joined together, let not man put asunder."

There is no stronger indictment that the Opium Eater could bring against rum and opium than their demoralizing and annulling conflictions against the most holy and divine institution of marriage.

To these unhallowed influences am I indebted for all my humiliation. Large cities are full of men and women living promiscuously together without divine or human sanction. The story of the Samaritan woman at the well could be duplicated many times in our most Puritanical cities. What wonder, then, that I am thus compelled to make confession in order that the caption to this chapter may be understood! At scarce twenty-two years of age, in violation of a law that will never go unpunished, I find myself transgressing the Divine injunction of the seventh commandment. As time passes on, a circumstance happens, and the woman lies upon a bed which she feels is that of death. In order to avoid disgrace to family ties, a marriage license is procured; the services of a clergyman (who, in this instance, thinks more of securing his fee than the solemn office he is about to perform), sanctions the marriage covenant in a few hurried words, while the dying woman is propped up in bed. At a request, he withholds the act from immediate publication. But her life does not go out. Opium, like liquor, gives an abandonment to the soul that makes it indifferent as to coming events. It lives in the present. It knows no tomorrow. Events soon transpire whereby wealth comes to her. Our transgression of law now confronts us in a new form; but with money at her command a divorce annuls her lawful marriage contract; and shortly after, during her last sickness, a civil representative of law repeats the words that make her the legal wife of the Opium Eater. Thus have I epitomized these events that the reader may comprehend the disconnected parts, and I trust I have made it simple and plain, that the last section of the heading— "the death of my wife"—may be understood.

"All's well that ends well." But this whole thing was wrong, from first to last. Such things ought not to be possible in one of the most enlightened commonwealths. Make divorcements hard to be obtained, and you make marriage more honorable; a solemnizer of the most sacred vows on earth above mercenary considerations.

*   *   *   *   *   *

This incident, one of the saddest and most painful in this narrative,— one I would gladly leave untold, but one that, I trust, will have more weight, more real power of diverting and strengthening the mind of those so foolishly or thoughtlessly inclined,— is a fitting culmination to the acts that must sooner or later follow those who violate the laws of God, whether they are ignorant of them or not. Do not think that this condition does not come by a single first indulgence. All the moral and physical wrecks everywhere to be seen were once in a state of innocence and purity, but a first indulgence could only have made it possible for their blighted lives and hopes.

The charms of social life, the seemingly innocent pleasures, the wine, and the trifling dissipations, and follies, and foibles of our lives, are too often the subtle, silken cords that, woven so carelessly and thoughtlessly, are constantly becoming coarser and more vulgar, until at last we find ourselves in bands of steel, and there comes back to us only mockings and jeers at all our feeble and hopeless struggles to break away from our captor — vicious habits.

During a period of time when I had the responsibility of providing for a home, and, feeling unable to conquer the gaming-table passion alone, I called to my assistance a lawyer acquaintance, and had myself placed in the position of a "kicker," where pride alone would restrain me from again visiting them. But in 1879, however, my wife having come into the possession of means sufficient to supply all her wants, I had, by a singular combination of circumstances, again fallen a victim to this seductive and most fascinating passion.

Passing along the street, one day, I met a kindly old

man whose life of toil had gone to satisfy his gambling mania. My old acquaintance, unconscious of doing me an injury, called my attention to a very "tony" gaming house just opened, where sumptuous dinners and choice liquors were daily served. Liquor, by the way, is always a free commodity in first-class gambling houses.

I passed on, not thinking of entering, nor having any desire to renew fellowship with my former captor, when my companion, — a younger brother, — expressed an inclination to see the "tiger," as the game of faro is sometimes called. Although a considerable lapse of time had intervened since my last appearance, the man at the "peek-hole" being satisfied that I was "all right," the massive door, made to withstand the battering sledge-hammer blows of the police for a season, swung noiselessly open, and the magnificently furnished "lair of the tiger" was in full view. I went in, heedless of danger, and merely to gratify the curiosity of my brother. The spirit of the slumbering past awoke, and in a short space of time what money I possessed had changed hands, and borrowing all my brother had, his soon followed mine into the box. It is an inevitable law of life that the individual who reforms from any habit and yields again to it, becomes far more dissipated and reckless than before. My case was no exception to the rule. I can give but a vague idea of the blindness of this passion during the next few months following this unfortunate occurrence. My wife was sick unto death. My days and nights were given up, to a large extent, ministering to her wants, and the despair incidental to her condition made me oblivious to my own. Antidotes and doctors were of no avail, and all earthly friends

"THE SPIRIT OF THE PLACE AND THE GAME FORSOOK ME."—(*page 45.*)

seemed to have fled; and, given over to the opium curse, life could only be kept alive by recourse to ether in conjunction with morphia.

On the morning of the 21st of April, 1880, after passing a night that had been made sad by the condition that my wife was in, and the impression that her end was near, but thinking that it was not immediate, I went out for a short respite. In my stroll I passed the gambling hell previously alluded to. I entered. I had played but a short time when, for the first time in all my experience at this fascinating, soul-destroying sport, the spirit of the place and the game forsook me. I stopped playing, "cashed in my chips," and left the place, and that, too, in the midst of what is termed a "deal." Never shall I forget the sensation of peace and freedom that came to me. It seemed as though I should never desire to gamble again —that the charm was broken, the spell had forever ended. I felt a longing desire to return to the sick chamber, and devote my life to the service of the dying soul. I took home with me a necessity from a drug store, and the only thing that she could relish to eat,— ice cream.

The servant opened the door to me. Asking after my wife during my short absence, I was told that she was sleeping, and admonished by a sign to make no noise to disturb her. As I entered the chamber softly all was quiet. She seemed to be sleeping. As I sat down, I noticed for the first time that the coverlet was drawn up over her face. After remaining a few moments I gently removed it. The face looked unusually calm and tranquil. I listened for the breathing. I found none.

The spirit had flown! I was alone in the presence of the dead!

*   *   *   *   *   *   *   *

One more scene, and I turn away from this sad picture of an uncompleted life, going out when it should have been most vigorous ; and, saddest of all, in such a manner.

A clergyman of distinction — sent by whom I know not — officiated at the funeral. My wife for years had disconnected herself from church membership. On the night preceding this sudden flight of the spirit, she spoke of her near approach to the portals of the unseen world, and longed for the touch of the tenderest hand on earth, —a mother's,—but there was none. She asked me to pray for her,— for myself, — but no clergyman did she desire. I believed in God,— in the Saviour of mankind. We all do. But I never prayed in those days, nor had I for years. I could not deny the plaintive petition, however, sinner though I was.

CHAPTER VI.

I ATTEMPT TO BREAK AWAY FROM THE OPIUM HABIT, DO
NOT SUCCEED, AND RETURN TO GAMBLING.

LEFT with sufficient property, on the death of my
wife, to have kept me for the remainder of my life
in comfort, my opium habit did not immediately
strike me as needing attention. The gambling mania was
again upon me, and I passed many of my waking hours
within the haunts of this and kindred sports, and followed
out the inclination of a man with no ambition or stated
purpose in life. Along in the summer months following
my wife's decease (1880), I determined to make an effort
to release myself from my opium habit. In New Hampshire there resided a physican who had an "antidote" for
the morphine habit. I had consulted him once before,
and he had been very frank and confidential with me on
that occasion. The patient, however, at that time, was
another person,— my wife. He told me then that it was
useless to try further for her; that she was beyond help;
that neither De Quincy nor any one else had ever left off
the use of the drug, and invited me to read De Quincy's
"Confessions," and also a work by Dr. Calkins on the
opium habit, both of which he loaned me. Alas! I did
not read them, however. · The latter book might have
been read with profit. At least, it would have shown me
the end of the road, as found by others, over which I was

fast traveling. But now things had changed, and I was in need of assistance. His formula, also, had undergone a change for the better,— they usually do in such cases,— and he thought by a strict conformity to his directions I would come out all right. I tried it, but I almost immediately abandoned it, as it did not sustain me. And yet, in a comparatively short space of time, I came to him again. And again, ashamed to be known by him, under an assumed name I consulted him. "Drowning men catch at straws." Opium users grasp false promises and delusive hopes almost to the very last.

I returned to Boston, and followed a still falser light, if possible,— the gaming table. In the toils of gamblers I put up a "bank roll," and with a finely furnished house in the residential portion of the city, banked a "private game," and on the "inside" saw the operation of the system of "protection," and how immunity from arrest and trouble is carried out by the paid guardians of the public weal. This book being more intimately associated with the Opium Eater's experiences with the drug, he leaves his gambling life for a more enlarged form.

I narrate an incident occurring while engaged in this unrighteous occupation, to show the potency of opium on the mind in cases of anxiety, and how indelibly fixed everything will remain in connection with it. During the early fall I went to Albany, N. Y., in company with my lecherous friends, with the double purpose of ": banking " a faro game and attending the races. Gambling seemed an uncheckable vice in that metropolis. It was nearly midnight; in my room at the Delevan House I dropped my hypodermic syringe upon the floor and the glass barrel was broken. This left me stranded, so to speak; and while I might have drank the drug, as many do, I preferred this more torturous way of injecting it under the skin. On account of the lateness of the hour, I apprehended I might have some trouble in getting the instrument and morphia, being a stranger in the city. Groundless fear. In all the years I had been associated with opium takers, in cities of several States, with statutory enactment severe and penalties large for violation of the law, and in innumerable drug stores, the Opium Eater never experienced any more difficulty in obtaining the drug than in buying the most harmless thing. Here it was simplicity itself. I met some one at that late hour with intelligence enough to direct me to such a place as I was looking for, and I easily found it. The druggist had drawn his curtains, to close. Asking in a calm and thoroughly familiar manner for the objects of my visit, and at the same time explaining in an offhand way my accident, he readily showed me his wares, and I as hastily purchased those I was in need of. He volunteered to me, in the conversation that ensued, the information that he had twelve opium patients to whom he daily administered the drug; and the terrible experiences of two others came up before my eyes, as I contemplated the aggregate amount of their misery. I have read since, from newspaper clippings, that Albany has been maligned, perhaps falsely, as having a large number of opium takers. Where are they not? But the effect of that midnight visit was so indelibly fixed on my mind, that although it was my first and only visit to that city, and years have since elapsed, the Opium Eater feels confident he could go from that hotel to that drug store blindfolded.

Much of the dark mystery which surrounds the manifestations of so-called mind-readers, mediums, and hypnotic influences, might be cleared away if one takes into consideration that the best manipulators of the "black art" are not infrequently the users to excess of drugs in some one of the many forms. They thus place themselves in a more placid or receptive state, and throw their powers unrestrained into their "guides'" control.

Anæsthetics, in the form of chloroform and ether, are frequently resorted to and prescribed in critical emergencies to enslaved opium victims; and I affirm whereof I know, when I say that disembodied evil spirits are their controlling power, whereas the "medium" may be largely ignorant of the source from whence they derive their manifestations. It was the intention of the Opium Eater to relate an experience under the mediumistic or hypnotic state produced by ether; an experience so full of evil spirits and mind torture; that I preferred to bear the ills of my cursed existence than resort to this mode of temporary relief ever after. He believes, however, that in stating its source, he renders as valuable a service as though he gave the experience; while, perhaps, on the other hand, it might throw a little light on so-called psychical phenomena.

Israel's king, when forsaken by God's prophet, went to the same unholy source for light, and in the soothsayer of Endor had revealed to him his own calamitous end. There is no God in these revealments from any point of view, and the code of morals established in Jesus Christ are largely ignored in practice if not in precept by those thus fortified in spiritualistic manifestations.

CHAPTER VII.

"WHO FELL AMONG THIEVES"—A STARTLING EXPERIENCE.

I RETURNED to Boston after my experience in putting up a "bank-roll" for faro at Albany, but not
without witnessing that delightful and soul-inspiring
panorama of nature lying between that city and New
York on the Hudson River, well-plucked of my money,
and thoroughly disgusted. The "game" had been profitable enough to every one save the Opium Eater. With a
$500 bank-roll, nearly $2,000 had flowed into the box during the short period of time that I watched the game. But
it "ran off," and I realized no increment. My property
had melted like snow before a burning sun ; and, while I
was not bent on money-getting, I found all my funds
swiftly flowing into the channel laid out for them by my
"friends." Everybody was kind. If I wanted a few
thousand dollars, and I consulted the man with $100,000
to loan on first-class security, he had it, provided everything was all right. Of course everything was all right.
But it cost the Opium Eater lots of money to prove his
case. Then, all things being proven satisfactorily to the
man with $100,000 strong, the inexperienced prodigal
received his money, less a princely commission to his supposed lender. To get a mortgage on one day, and off the

next, so to speak, came hard on the estate, but as long as there was money in it, at fabulous rates of interest, every one was satisfied to be inconvenienced. What a lot of vultures they were! My case is no exception to that of innumerable others. Men live, or rather exist, their sole object in life being to look out for the young man with money or inherited wealth ; and these scavengers of the human race are on hand to cater to their every inclination, in whatever direction they may lie. Many pay the highest price for that which is the most shallow in the way of pleasure, and if they only knew what was behind it they would turn away from it with intense disgust. While I was thoughtlessly putting up my money to back gambling schemes, and thereby digging a pit for my fellow-man, I was having it made ready for myself by my pretended friends. I had shown to me by a gambler the devices for cheating. They were marvelous in mechanism and ingenuity. Yet the novice thinks he is getting a " square deal," and rarely ever is undeceived. A gentleman with a periodical mania for gaming, entered his well-equipped establishment to "buck" the game. He had $1500. "I did not have a dollar to my name. But, with a good man as assistant, I did not waste any time winning the first $400 or $500. After that I played with him as the cat plays with a mouse, —I dragged him through long hours, and left him broke and exhausted at one and the same time." I saw two men lose several hundred dollars where it would have been impossible for them to have won more than ten in cash. Men are continually losing far greater sums where it would not be possible to win even a dollar. Yet the surroundings and appearances are "gilt-edged."

"A gambler has no need to carry a gun," said a professional one to me, after two of his class had forfeited their lives in a Boston gambling house, "for the reason that he never attempts to cheat any one except those he can do so to without fear of detection." But they are not infallible in this particular, as these two lives testified.

The last few months had convinced me that I had had enough of the "inside" of a gambler's life, although I did not see things then as I do now. It was ill luck with me then. It is robbery now. The minions of the law, not being able to levy and collect one of their "protection" licenses, took the paraphernalia and disposed of it all, — not as the law requires, by destruction, but for a cash consideration to professional gamblers. I found myself, however, still possessed of some $2,000 in cash and personal property, together with my team; and, gathering up the remnants, I returned to the home of my youth and my grandfather, where my mother was then living.

I do not think one would have taken me for a desperately dissipated man. I looked more like an invalid, — without being one,— pale, thin, and emaciated. One day, in passing along a crowded thoroughfare the Opium Eater felt a hand gently laid on his shoulder, and words like these saluted him from the lips of a dapper young fellow whose face he had become familiar with in gaming houses: "You and I are the subject of a wager. So-and-so bet a bottle of wine that you would 'pass in your checks' (die) first," and he smilingly went his way. They did not have long to wait. He died shortly after. I occupied my time principally in sleeping (to the great annoyance of my grandsire), reading, driving, and fighting the opium habit. At this

time I again consulted my New Hampshire doctor (a gentleman, by the way), and received encouraging advice and
a bottle of his antidote medicine. But it proved a rope of
sand ; and after a few trials I put it away in my chamber
closet. It was a few days before Christmas, 1880, that I
met with an experience that thoroughly aroused me, and
made me determined, at whatever cost and suffering, to
abandon this habit. It was after the noon hour, and retiring to my chamber I took a "hypo" of morphine. In inserting the needle in my left leg, it entered a large vein or
an artery. In an instant the contents of the syringe —
thirty minims of the strongest solution of morphia — was
in the channels of my blood. I flew to my feet in a wild
state. The sensation is indescribable. I flung the instrument away. Dashing to the window I partly raised it,
with the intention of throwing myself into the huge bank
of snow underneath it, all the while frantically sending
my hands through my hair, the sensation and pressure on
the brain was so terrible. But I controlled the impulse.
Hurrying down through the house I entered the barn, and
divesting myself of my coat and vest (for a flame as hot
and fierce as that raging in Tophet seemed to have suddenly enveloped me), I walked and walked the barn floor,
in the cold, piercing December atmosphere. The length
of time I thus walked I know not. It seemed as though I
was wrapped and swayed in blankets full of needles, which
were being driven into my brain, and the soles of my feet,
and through every pore of my skin incessantly. When
the reaction came, however, I was translated to "Green-
land's icy mountains," and I shivered and shook like an
aspen leaf, and my teeth rattled together in an uncontrol-

"I WALKED, AND WALKED THE BARN FLOOR IN THE COLD, PIERCING
DECEMBER ATMOSPHERE."—(*page 54.*)

able manner. I sought the house, all unconscious that any of its inmates, especially my dear mother, knew I was a victim to opium. To them, I simply had had a chill. The little stove, although driven to its utmost capacity, failed to throw out heat sufficient to penetrate me, though I almost hugged it in my eagerness to catch its warmth. Hot "composition" failed to bring about the desired end, and the fact that I was domiciled in a "temperance town" give rise to no thoughts of spirituous liquors to quicken the inner parts with its fiery flame. The fear and terror of again resorting to the treacherous demon to help me out was simply agonizing. Strange, too, I did not think of drinking it. I retired early, and high were the comfortables that were piled upon me to produce warmth. Not, however, until after cautiously taking a "hypo" of the drug did I fall asleep. When I awoke, after a disordered sleep, it seemed as though I must be in a lake of water, so drenched was I from perspiration. Everything I had taken, together with the large load of quilts, had simply given me in my weakness a tremendous sweat. I was sick for several days from this experience.

CHAPTER VIII.

I ENTER THE MAINE GENERAL HOSPITAL AS A PATIENT.

IN THE morning I was more determined than ever to fight the last battle for freedom under medical treatment, and, at the proper time, I made my appearance at the office of the Maine General Hospital, in Portland, Me. The resident physician received me kindly, and to him I confided my condition. We talked the whole matter over calmly, as physicians with honorable and conscientious purposes usually do, and I related my connection with the drug. He did not give me an immediate answer, but requested me to call the next day, when a final decision would be made to me. I was accepted, and entered upon my treatment. My attending physician was one well known to me, and acquainted with my family. While I did not make myself known, he undoubtedly knew me as well as I did him. He was, like all the others, a gentleman,— kind, courteous, and sympathetic, and did everything that human ingenuity, and thought, and practice could devise. He examined me daily, and seemingly took great personal interest in the case. I felt I was safe, and in honorable hands. He was very frank in his manner, and asked me if I had any of the drug concealed about me, and at the same time volunteered the remark that "opium takers were the most infernal liars on the face of the earth," or words of similar import,— words that are no doubt true, when relating to their expedients for obtaining opium. He then reasoned how useless it would be for me to make the attempt without a complete surrender, and not to practice deception. Still, I felt nervous and fearful, and I confess I did have some of the drug, as well as a hypodermic syringe, secreted about me. I was afraid I might get where they could not feel for my infirmities, and I felt I could trust no man absolutely and entirely with my soul. But after a few days, when confidence had been begotten, in a burst of trustfulness I gave my instruments to the house doctors as presents, exposing myself thereby to duplicity, and stood on their good offices. It was the intention and desire of the Opium Eater to have incorporated here the daily record of the case as kept by the hospital; but in this year of grace 1893, in visiting the institution and conferring with the physician in charge, and also with one of my attending doctors, I found that the rules of the hospital forbade their being copied out of the records unless by consent of the trustees.

"The fact that the treatment did not effect a cure, would make them valueless to medical practitioners," said the resident physician. " We never attempt nowadays to deal with that class of patients. It is useless. Our conveniences and the institution is not adapted for them."

It was this same gentleman who said to the Opium Eater, on one occasion, that "my deliverance from the power of opium he considered as great a miracle as ever was performed in the days of Christ."

The result of this treatment, as it is recalled after more than a dozen years, was of incalculable service to me. I found under restraint that a far smaller quantity of the drug answered the purpose better than the amount I had been using.   When I entered the hospital I was using more than three hundred drops of saturate solution of morphine a day, besides what liquor I drank, to say nothing of the excessive use of tobacco.   Far less in quantity to what many others consumed, but the physique and temperament have much to do with its use by different individuals. My physicians reduced what I was daily taking two-thirds at the start,— or one hundred, — and at the same time reduced the strength relatively.   This was readily made manifest to the Opium Eater by the smarting or burning sensation caused by the additional amount of water added. Then the reduction was kept up at one drop less at each " hypo,"—or three drops a day graduation.

For a while things improved wonderfully. Life seemed returning, and an activity hitherto bound or restrained, sprang into existence.   But peculiar feelings began shortly to manifest themselves.   My lungs sent forth pains, a cough appeared, and in my loins and limbs pains unknown before annoyed me.   Although in a comparatively small room, heated by steam, I could not keep warm.   Slight chills would follow each other at intervals, as light gusts of wind blew the snow from my window sills.   As the drug was lessened, and the vast quantities of opium began working out of the tissues of my system, all these symptoms were augmented ; and while I fought on, and hoped ever, the agony was simply intense.   My very limbs seemed as though they would snap and break, and were not unlike in feeling what in my youth were called " growing pains," but greatly intensified.   The only relief that came to me was when my doctor administered the morphia or my nurse rubbed my aching limbs in alcohol. But such reliefs were temporary only. I tried to occupy my time in reading during the earlier stages of my self-inflicted incarceration. I found one volume in the hospital library which I read to no great spiritual profit, or edification, or thoughtful purpose in a Christian sense, entitled " Fox's Book of Martyrs ;" a work which, while it glorifies the Christian faith, condemns the Church as not being in the faith of its peerless Founder and head.

But little cared the Opium Eater for those things then. He felt and realized that he was already in torment. To show how a man will sometimes suffer needlessly, and surrender his self-knowledge to those who know less than he does, I recall an incident in this connection. By sad and painful experience the morphine user finds where he can, and where he cannot, insert this needle of torture in his body. This duty devolved upon a very agreeable young student, who, like many youth, thought he knew more about this matter than he did. Of course I was the patient, and must submit to ignorance and his practice. He did all the inserting of the needle, and very often I would tell him not to put it where he thought he ought to. On one occasion, putting it too close to the muscles of the kneejoint, I informed him that he would surely bring an abscess if he put it there. He knew better, however. But the abscess came, and I bore the pain while he scientifically treated it, taking nearly double the time experience had taught me to effect a cure. Otherwise, he was very considerate, and treated the Opium Eater with gentlemanly courtesy and unvarying kindness.

But now toward the end of my stay, matters began to grow desperate with me. The most distressing symptoms were the pains in my limbs and the hot and cold flushes that swept over my body. I ate scarcely anything, but nauseation soon followed the meals. My restlessness was something beyond description. The hours of the day, from 8 A. M. to 8 P. M., with three allowances of the drug, together with the use of tobacco, I managed to live. The nights were different. Time had come to an end. I have heard the clock strike the midnight hour, and waited, — and waited,— and perhaps fell asleep, and thought it must be near morning,— and waited another seemingly endless period of time, and when the joyous sound of the stroke of the clock came floating through the frosty midnight air, and attentively I count, — one, I think that, perhaps, I am not awake, or I heard only the last stroke of a later hour, and I slip out of bed, in a room as hot as steam and steampipes can make it, and shiver and shake, and ask the nurse — who seems to have taken sufficient time to circumnavigate the earth before he reappears — the hour, and find, alas! that my ears have not deceived me if my other senses have. These scenes cannot be overdrawn! The sleep — if it can be called by so sweet a name — is of that nature that a few moments of it seems endless. One feels as though he were continually struggling, as in a nightmare, to throw off the powers that are holding and dragging him down ; and when finally released, his tongue seems thick, and the eyes and head and body not unlike the sensation produced by the condition of one's foot or limb being "asleep"— a stoppage of the circulation. I made the attempt during these last remain-

ing days in the hospital to try and substitute with a little
alcoholic stimulant; and to this end I procured a bottle
of rum, brought to me by a young man who was an out-
patient at the hospital, and who obtained it from one of
the "kitchen" barrooms of my prohibitory city. My
nurse, however, discovered it, and reasoned me out of in-
dulging in it. So acute did I become that I could readily
discern among all the employees and others the footsteps
of my student practitioner. Highly amusing it was to
him as he noted my earnestness and pleasure at his coming. He knew it was not so much himself that the Opium
Eater was so particularly interested in as the few "drops"
of morphia he carried. I noted where everything that
in any way had bearing in the way of relief was kept,—
the morphine for the use of patients, and where my nurse
had placed in his trunk a new and an unused hypodermic
syringe, a gift to him. I had now come down to close
range with my tormentor, and as a last resort made use of
my knowledge. No other picture presents itself to my
mind, of a descriptive character, to portray my feelings,
other than that of a fish taken from his elements. He
lies floundering and gasping by turns, as though trying
to find that which will resuscitate its life. In these terrible straits, thief-like, I made descents for both opium
closet and my nurse's syringe, entering his room, and even
going to his trunk and taking it out. Thus armed, I
would return hurriedly to my room, and desperately and
wickedly bare the flesh and plow the needle in, regardless
of consequences. But I only did this a few times. I reasoned: I am the most interested party to this transac-
tion. I may deceive others, but not myself. So, abruptly,

one morning, after some thirty days' treatment, I gave notice, with some false excuse, that I was going, and bidding my attendants good-bye, summarily left.

"Not cured!" is the record on the hospital books. But I had not abandoned the idea of overcoming this habit. I intended moving the battlefield and fighting it out alone, far away from any temptation to be dishonest, and where I could not get the drug.

Apropos of my nurse. Jokingly he would try on my coats, and approvingly admire their fit; tell me of the patients who had recently passed away on my couch, and other interesting stories adapted to my nervousness. But he was most taken up with a "diamond" the Opium Eater wore in his shirt front. "All that glisters is not gold," nor diamonds that send forth sparkling and fiery lights. While I felt that I should have future use for my clothing, I placed no value on the Rhinestone that adorned my shirt front. He was very faithful in administering alcoholic ablutions to my aching limbs, and I trust the "diamond" glitters as brilliantly on his bosom front as on the morning he put on.

It was in the early morning hour a few days before my departure from the hospital, while intently watching for an opportunity to sally forth unobserved and purloin the drug, that I heard a voice through the half-open door, say: "My God! Am I to die here all alone!" What consolation there would have been, even in the presence of a stranger, at such an hour! How gladly would I have changed places with my unknown fellow-sufferer, and thus put an end to my physical misery. A short while after, hurrying feet passing my door told me he was at rest!

CHAPTER IX.

I ATTEMPT TO FIGHT THE DEMON MORPHIA SINGLE-HANDED AND AM DEFEATED.

I WENT from the hospital to my grandfather's in the country. I took no morphia, no liquor. I had given away all my hypodermic syringes to the medical students. Alone in this to me then bleak place, and cold and comfortless house,—to one that required so much heat,—I purposed continuing the battle with my terrible and uncompromising foe. The doctor had given me a tonic when I left the hospital,—a simple affair, I suppose,—for my appetite. There was no stimulating effects in it, however, that I now recall. I do not remember how the first day was passed. The morphine I had surreptitiously taken, together with the doctor's parting "hypo," had enabled me to get along through the day comfortably easy, but the early hours of the night I shall not forget in this world,—perhaps not in the one to come.

The old-fashioned "air-tight" stove in my chamber was filled with wood, and the room could be kept comfortably warm, provided one kept the stove well filled. But it burned rapidly, and roared annoyingly, and I had no fireman. Bedclothing, however, I had in profusion.

The terrible symptoms I have already described commenced early,—restlessness beyond description. My

brother, who occupied the bed with me, and who was so
familiar with my habit, would often say, "For God's
sake, Hen (the short for Henry), can't you keep still a
minute?" And then, with all the power of a supreme
effort, I would gather myself together, and find a position
where I believed I could rest for a long time. But almost
instantly he would say that I had not been still two minutes, when it seemed to me to have been many. I would
get so nervous trying to restrain myself, that I shall leave
a description of it to the witnesses I have introduced in
this work to do it for me.

I have previously alluded to an antidote from a New
Hampshire physician that I had tried, and discarded as
not being requisite. That, together with a bottle of the
extract of cocoa, were in a closet in the room. The latter
had been prescribed by a neighbor physician, and was as
useless in my case as water. The antidote, however, was
more powerful, and a tablespoonful was considered a dose
at the time it had been prepared for me sufficient to replace the large quantity of morphia I was then taking. I
did not stop for measurements now! I would slip out of
bed into the cold air, take a mouthful, and wait the result.
After taking several swallows I found sleep. The next
day was full of excruciating agony, and the night following was a repetition of the first. I tried to stop the terrible pains in my limbs with a bag of steeped hops, but they
proved of no avail. The black, heavy, liccorice-like antidote was the only thing sufficient to woo Morpheus, the
fickle god of sleep.

When I left the hospital I supposed that I had burned
completely the barriers behind me in this vain attempt for

freedom, and the unthought-of and until now forgotten one had proved a temporary saviour. Now I must retrace my hasty action, and resurrect, at least, some one of the many powerful opium drugs or stimulants to take the place of this form of using morphine. I did not give the matter that consideration I might, perhaps, under less trying circumstances, and I chose the one least likely to succeed — the alcoholic stimulant of whiskey. Who but an opium eater can conceive of the state of mind and body that I was in in this comparatively short lapse of time without having the morphine subcutaneously injected? The "antidote" failed to relieve the frightful pains in my limbs, and produced no calm and tranquil state of mind. The pictures on the walls exasperated me in their steady and fixed staring, and the Opium Eater had them summarily removed from the room, so tormenting were they, but in the presence of the living I fought a fight for self-control and concealment.

On the third day after leaving the hospital, I took the first train from Portland for Boston. The weather was exceedingly cold, and my warm clothing seemingly added nothing to my comfort. I felt miserable indeed, and greatly depressed. Of course liquor was the only thing outside of morphia known to me that would fire the blood and give life inspiring impulses. Arriving in Boston, I drank frequently of hot Irish and Scotch whiskeys, without the effect usually obtainable; and not until eleven o'clock at night, in one of Boston's most popular hostelries,— where the Opium Eater was known, perhaps, more from the eccentricity of his always asking for a room wellheated, than for any other distinguishing mark,— he passed

the remaining hours before daylight, the liquor having at
last given him what might be termed a "natural feeling."
Stupor came, but it did remain long. The early morning
hours found me in a state of existence where liquor could
not be retained and nauseation and sickness indescribable.

At the first ray of hope of finding a surgical instrument
establishment and a drug store open, I sallied forth for a
hypodermic syringe and a bottle of morphia. Why attempt to describe the relief afforded by this most potent
of drugs? And how? Were you ever hungry, — real
hungry,—when hours had been lengthened into days without food, and then feasted to satiety? I have been ; and
yet it could not be compared to the influence and satisfying results attained by this drug at this time. If it left
me in Hades, and did not exalt me to Paradise, it made me
once more an inhabitant of this terrestrial sphere. It
was not unlike putting on warm wool garments and sitting
before a blazing fire or basking in the sunshine, after being
taken from the freezing river, or naked, and cold, and exposed to bleak and cutting winds. But, alas, it was only
transitory !

The Opium Eater quotes a few lines from De Quincy
to corroborate the feeling accompanying the return to his
master, and for the occasion, appropriates them to himself :
"For it seemed to me as if then, first, I stood at a distance,
and aloof from the uproar of life; as if the tumult, the
fever, and the strife, were suspended ; a respite granted
from the secret burdens of the heart ; a sabbath of repose ; a resting from human labors. Here were the hopes
which blossom in the paths of life, reconciled with the
peace which is in the grave ; motions of the intellect as

unwearied as the heavens, yet for all anxieties a halcyon
calm ; a tranquility that seemed no product of inertia, but
as if resulting from mighty and equal antagonisms ; infinite activities, infinite repose.   O just, subtle, and mighty
Opium !"   *   *   *   *   *

The strong man who criticises my yielding again to the
seductive influence of morphia, has my sympathy.   I see
so many of them at every turn of life who are giants in
their own strength, capable of overcoming everything but
their own vanity and weaknesses, that they remind one of
the barking of small dogs, whom no sensible person takes
notice of, having learned by so doing that it only increases
the noise, and affords the nuisance the recognition it is
striving to obtain.

I had made the effort, and ignominiously failed.   I did
not, however, brood over my defeat.   The suffering I had
undergone had satisfied me, and no doubt would have
brought from the Opium Eater a like laudation of morphia
(had he been like gifted) that De Quincy paid to laudanum, when he almost deified the demon of our combined
destruction, in the language following.   After stating that
twice he had, for some time, entirely abandoned the use
of opium and again resumed its indulgence, he thus con-
cludes :—

"During this third prostration before the dark idol, and
after some years, new phenomena began slowly to arise.
For a time these were neglected as accidents or palliated
by such remedies as I knew of.   But when I could no
longer conceal from myself that these dreadful symptoms
were moving forward forever, by a pace steadily, solemnly,
and equably increasing, I endeavored, with some feeling

of panic, for a third time to retrace my steps. But I had not reversed my motion for many weeks before I became profoundly aware that this was impossible. Or, in the imagery of my dreams, which translated everything into their own language, I saw, through vast avenues of gloom, those towering gates of ingress, which hitherto had always seemed to stand open, now at last barred against my retreat and hung with funeral crape. The sentiment which attends the sudden revelation that all is lost! silently is gathered up into the heart; it is too deep for gestures or for words; and no part of it passes to the outside. Were the ruin conditional, or were it in any point doubtful, it would be natural to utter ejaculations, and to seek sympathy. But where the ruin is understood to be absolute, where sympathy cannot be consolation, and counsel cannot be hope, this is otherwise. The voice perishes; the gestures are frozen; and the spirit of man flies back upon its own center. I, at least, upon seeing those awful gates closed and hung with draperies of woe, as for a death already past, spoke not, nor started, nor groaned. One profound sigh ascended from my heart, and I was silent for days."

My break from my fond hope acted as it acts on all humanity. I drifted more rapidly than ever toward its quicksands and my final doom. My gambling mania returned; and, like the periodical drunkard, during the next few months I variated between the two cities, infatuated with the vice more cursed, if possible, than opium itself, until I saw go into the coffers of the gambling hells every dollar of ready money that I possessed; and, as a fitting climax, my horses and carriages were sacrificed on the same unholy altar,— so suddenly, indeed, and the greater part of it at one play, that early in the summer the Opium Eater found himself a "broke" man, in purse as well as in spirit and in health.

Under these circumstances my habits did not improve. I lived, I do not vividly recall how. I returned East for the summer, after losing the remnant of my money, to the home of my good grandparent, but the prodigal did not receive a prodigal's reception. I was a gentleman in appearance (if goodly apparel betokens the man), if not always in action; but, alas! that which is stigmatized "the root of all evil," I was dispossessed of. I now consider that it was right that the Opium Eater should be invited to "move on" and out, for it was a rigid part of the old gentleman's religious convictions that "he that will not work, neither shall he eat," and, to use a scriptural phrase, his "heart was hardened" against me; by whom or what I shall not endeavor to say, but I was invited to seek shelter elsewhere.

In my profligacy, however, but a short time before, I had parted with much of my household effects to a woman who was desirous of making a home for herself and little ones, and whose residence was in the adjoining city; and hither I sought shelter. But a man without money ought not to expect that those equally poor should provide for him; but such is the blighting and destroying effect of opium and alcohol upon our humanity that all sense of right and justice deserts us.

I lived by pawning my valuables and selling various effects of a household character. My wants were few and easily supplied,— opium and alcoholic stimulants being the

principal ones.   My time — that which was not passed in
sleep — was wasted in some one of Portland's numerous
low groggeries, where a prohibitory law had failed to ex-
terminate the most damnable form of drinking hells on
earth.   Here, again, in my temporary shelter, the Divine
injunction that the unearned morsel shall be withheld from
the idle and shiftless, followed me ; and actions, more manifest than words, compelled me to again move on and out,
although on a fair and equitable basis my friends were
my debtors.   But there are times when arguments are useless, and these times usually appear when the individual
is the least prosperous.   On the whole, however, I have
no doubt I was treated far better than I deserved.

As before stated, while stopping in Portland the Opium
Eater passed most of his days in some one of these
kitchen barrooms of his native city, where he saw some of
the worst phases of the drinking habit.   The associations
were of the lowest.   Guilt, and vice, and misery shrink as
by a natural instinct from the public gaze ; they covert
privacy and solitude ; and even in the choice of a grave,
will sometimes sequester themselves from the general population of the churchyard, as if declining to claim even
fellowship with the great family of man, and wishing, in
the affecting language of Wordsworth, —

> " Humbly to express
> A penitential loneliness."

And stored away in some quiet nook of the barroom I
passed my time, taking no part in the general jargon of
the place, but alive to the goings on and doings of the
loiterers.   It was here, one afternoon, that one of those

slick gentry who live from off the lack of knowledge of those whom they find congregated in such places, was robbing a sailor by his handicraft at cards. The sailor, at last maddened by drink and the imposition being practiced upon him, resented the conspirator's game. He was alone among a half dozen conscienceless villians, and the Opium Eater, perceiving that a squall was about to break, moved toward the door; but before reaching it its fury was at its height. The sailor backed slowly out, fighting his antagonists with whatever lay within his reach, and barroom crockery flew about in all directions; and with fierce oaths and demolishing glassware, the fearful thumping of these maddened demons in a barroom fight at close range was an ugly and terrifying spectacle. Finally, landed through the door by superior numbers, the sailor turned upon his victors, and with lightning-like motions a knife was whipped from his pocket, and it being unseen by his victorious enemies, he rushed upon them with determined and murderous intent. He makes but one lunge, and one of his tormentors falls within the door. No cry is heard; the door shuts, and the sailor walks calmly but rapidly away. Standing but a few paces from the stricken man, I see the act in all its horrible detail; but so quickly does it transpire that speech is not framed soon enough to give warning. The man is seriously wounded,—disemboweled, almost; but by holding the aperture together until a physician can be called to stitch it up, he saves his life. The sailor is arrested; his victim survives. The Opium Eater is summoned to court as a witness, and although persuaded by the barroom gang to be agreed as to the cause of the disturbance, — and, of course, the sailor was to be the aggressor,— he preferred to state the facts as he eye-witnessed them. The liquor-cursed sailor, by as close a shave as any man ever came to being an unintentional murderer, gets six months in the common jail.

As by a thread, two lives hung by so simple, and worse than foolish, an act as barroom tippling. But there was no moralizing lesson in it to the Opium Eater in those hopeless and abandoned days. It is a common, every-day occurrence all over our fair land.

During these weeks or months,— my recollection fails me as to time,— I have no remembrance of visiting the only true friend I had on earth, my mother. Only a few miles separated us. No feeling of anger or resentment toward my aged and respected grandparent restrained me. I remember no farewell parting when I took my final departure from the city. An institution born with such hideous deformities as the saloon, that robs man of his manhood, that causes him to forget motherhood, to look down and not up, to sink into nothingness all righteous aspirations, ought to be obliterated from the face of the earth !

CHAPTER X.

A DISHONORABLE LAWYER — I ADVOCATE MY OWN CASE.

AGAIN the Opium Eater finds himself in Boston's great heart,— not good heart,— under circumstances too long to detail here, whether or not to his credit ; but he found himself again in the toils of his professed friends,— gambling friends,— engaged in contesting under legislative enactments, the results of an unlawful life. I now became as familiar an object in the haunts of the disciples of Blackstone, as I had before been in the weird and fascinating temples of King Faro. I was being used, however, simply as the cat's-paw to pull the golden chestnuts from the pockets of professional gamblers and transfer them to the "leathers" of those souless and dishonorable-honorable gentlemen—my attorneys.

Why further draw the picture of my degradation and misery, so familiar to the eye of every observant student of human nature? That the world is full of like fallen beings, characterized under various titles and names, and classed as hopeless and irredeemably lost, may be sufficient reason. Let me, then, give you the picture as drawn by the young barrister who pleaded my cause for his own good and gain, and whose tragic end showed me more clearly, more forcibly than revelation itself, that the man who robs widows, and orphans, and profligates, and the hireling, of their just dues and their wages, may, and more often does, escape the statutory law therefor, but he does not escape that law which is eternal, which is just, and which grinds its transgressors to humiliation, and often to death. I have seen sufficient to convince me that no man can rob his fellows and escape punishment. The canceled debt of slavery cost a fearful aggregate in whatever way it is viewed.

This man, in a plea for justice in my behalf before a jury, used language like this: "I do not desire to shield the character and reprehensible habits of my client. I have no doubt that the years he has spent at the gaming-table has made of him a worthless wreck — physically and financially." That these words might have their full weight and effect upon the jury, he had arranged to place the Opium Eater in an unoccupied part of the courtroom (the witness benches); where, seated alone and in close proximity to the jurymen, my counsel, with dramatic effect, pointed his finger toward me, and with tragic fervency completed the picture he had so faithfully drawn,—clothed as I was in "filthy garments," and wasted and emaciated in body by my excesses and poverty. And yet, while he gave me no character, Judas-like, he had the price of his perfidy and his villainy in his pocket; and, unless the Opium Eater has been misinformed, a like tragic end befell him that came to the unfortunate Judas, and also to one of more modern date, one Piggott, a forger and perjurer, who for gold made the unsuccessful attempt to destroy the cause and character of Charles Stewart Parnell, the Irish constitutional agitator,— suicide.

I might multiply this incident by others similar in character, but not with so tragic a result, however. I place it

here for the purpose of serving a double end in this case
— it gives you a not overdrawn picture of the Opium
Eater at this time [1882] on the one hand ; and a moral on
the other — never rob the helpless.

I am not depicting a saint in myself ; far from it. But
a man can be a sinner and yet have his skirts clean from
the infamy of robbing or injuring innocence. I plead
guilty that the whole course pursued by myself in suing
for the recovery of money not won on the "square," may
have been wrong in a manly sense, and the " baby act,"
but it was inaugurated and carried out in its inception by
gamblers, who held me before them as a shield. The State
enacted the law for a wise and good purpose, and no reason exists why this lawyer should do the highwayman act,
even in dealing with unprincipled men, and wrest from
them the money, and then withhold every penny of it from
the hapless victim of an uncontrollable mania, by treachery and duplicity. Twelve men readily assented to the
righteousness of the case, and the highest court of the Com-
monwealth affirmed their decree ; yet this lawyer stood,
wolf-like, between justice and right, and confident that
with me a few months, at most, must bring my earthly existence to a close, intended by his act to hasten my departure as soon as possible, by withholding that which alone,
seemingly, could prolong it—money. Ah ! my friends,
innocently, blindly, and ignorantly I pursued this *ignis-
fatuus* for months—the last beacon of light and ray of hope
to help me out of my miserable existence.

Chapters might be written on these men and my dealings
with them ; and how, finally, appealing as a last resort to
Benjamin F. Butler, and he accepting the case, I felt that

I had an avenging Nemesis upon their tracks ; but death claiming them and him, the final appeal will come before that tribunal where gold will not tempt, and complete justice will be meted out to all.

However, after my emancipation, my startled lawyer friend fell back on the comforting morsel which, in conversation with me one day, he gave expression to by stating that "I had neither money nor friends, and what could I do about it ?" referring to that of which conscience was his accuser,—his duplicity. I held court, so to speak, for a few minutes, and was the advocate of my own cause, and he, together with several of his lawyer friends present, gave me as respectful attention as I expect ever to have accorded me in this world, until I had finished my plea, and the only exception noted was made by my former advocate. He said that I was "mad." "Much learning doth make thee mad," Festus said to Paul. "Much injustice and treachery hath made thee mad !" this man might have said with a large degree of truth. The madness which possessed my soul came not from hatred of the individual, but rather from the pent-up and bursting flame of injustice as I saw the truth of the position.

John Randolph of Roanoke being asked on one occasion where in his varied experience he had heard the greatest eloquence—he having been the Democratic leader of the House of Representatives, afterwards chosen United States Senator from Virginia, and in 1830 Minister to Russia — replied, "From a woman's lips on the slave-block in Virginia." The mind can easily frame a picture to fit so fearful a case,— separation from loved ones, perhaps father and mother, sister and brother, and, above all, husband and children. I candidly reviewed our connections, and made as clear and as explicit a summing up of his broken promises of a professed friendship as the inspiration of language could convey. No oaths, no curses, but the simple yet powerful truth, as drawn from the picture of my past wretchedness, of my condition and my hopelessness at a time when he alone had held out hope and financial salvation, and buoyed me up with false promises when he had already realized on the actions at law.

Not unlike the few opium eaters who have left their thoughts behind them, I had an intense longing to hide myself from the world in general, and my acquaintances in particular, and, in a seclusion far removed from the haunts of men, live out the remaining days of my life in Selkirk solitude. In my wanderings in better and happier days, although an opium eater, I had come upon a romantic spot that, in those days of expectancy in money matters, if they had been realized, would have shut me out from the unsympathetic world, from which I only cared to escape, and have placed me far away from my then present scenes of degradation and poverty. It was located in New Hampshire, and was on what is termed an "abandoned farm."

Is it too much to say that with a redemption of humanity, the "abandoned" homesteads will again resound with the joyous scenes of life as when they were exchanged by their occupants for the crowded city's struggling poverty and tenement house existence?

CHAPTER XI.

HOW I WAS LIVING.

TO DESCRIBE how the Opium Eater lived in those days, would be to write a separate volume. I shudder as I look back to the rookeries that gave me shelter. They were not Christian institutions, but rather those occupied by the courtezan and the abandoned, and that without any hope of reward. They, too, were cursed with weaknesses and infirmities not unlike my own ; and who shall say that the feeling that "makes one wonderous kind" was not theirs ?

My fight, too, with the gamblers had drawn their enmity upon me, and I heard through a friend, whose husband was engaged in the liquor business, that I was being shadowed by certain officers, who intended to "run me in" if they could find sufficient excuse, or find me intoxicated. Nothing, perhaps, in those days had a more terrifying effect upon the Opium Eater than that arising from the fear of the inhumanity I might be made to undergo from a lack of knowledge possessed by them of my habit, and the general indifference manifested by those constantly coming in contact with misery and wretchedness brought on and through a fast life. Hence I was not partial to a "lock-up" experience under such conditions.

Other circumstances also conspired against me, and I left that section of the city where I had started and completed so swift a destruction. I made various attempts to labor at my occupation, but my opium condition was always a source of hindrance. Another, wherein I was at great disadvantage, was the spirit of avarice and greed in those giving me employment, making me its victim. I have on more than one occasion faithfully worked long hours for employers whose professions of Christ's religion and piety seemed, at least, to guarantee a faithful performance of so trifling a matter as the low rate of wages that they had stipulated to pay. They were in most cases in spirit and in deed, if not in words, like unto my professional friend who had remarked, "No money and no friends; what are you going to do about it?"

I am not going into details, further than to say that as my circumstances became more and more limited my habit underwent a radical change. There was one thing I must always have,— morphine. Everything had to give way to this one essential of my life. But it was used far more sparingly and niggardly than in my more affluent days. I now began to profit by my hospital experience, and I kept myself under more rigid restriction. I had decreased the amount per diem far below the days of my prodigality.

But to resume the thread of my narrative. Inspired by the hope that my cases at law would yield a recompense, as I had obtained verdicts to the amount of several thousand dollars, I was permitted to find shelter from the elements with those whom I had known under more favorable conditions. Everything of value that I possessed was in the pawnbroker's hands. None but those who have actually come under poverty's direst curse can comprehend the Opium Eater's situation. I often slept at

two extremes,—the cellar or the attic.   My dining hours
were irregular, and far apart, and often meager at that.
Morphine and liquor were my mainstays.   I was constantly
growing weaker, and this precarious existence, without the
actual necessities of life,—food, clothing, home,—a veritable outcast, a stranger to everything like civilization,—
told sadly on my physical nature.   My flesh had melted
away, and my skin had become hard and dry, and clung
tenaciously to the muscles and bones, and the ordeal of
injecting morphine under the skin became a most excruciating and agonizing one, only attained by the most painful experience.   There seemed no way of relief from this
slow torture, from the fact that my means were so limited,
and money without stint would have been required for
providing more comfortable substitutes.   In this "winter
of my discontent" and humiliation, days would be passed
without regular meals, and I subsisted on what I gathered
from the barroom free-lunch counter and the cheapest
of cheap restaurants ; except, perhaps, when I had the
good fortune of picking up a few dollars by meeting some
one I had befriended in other days, when I lived on the
best while it lasted, and took the cheapest when it was
exhausted.

The Opium Eater never kept a diary, but finds this in a
blank book, which by some chance seems to have followed
me to this late date.   It reads thus :—

OCTOBER 25, 1882.— My God ! what shall I do ?   Shall
I take my life on this beautiful night ?   Penniless and
hungry,—no money, and no work, and no health.   My
God ! Save me ! Save this poor wreck,—if it is thy will.
Deliver me from this hour,—this cold, dark and dreary

winter. Save this image in the likeness of thy Son, and make good to come from this the darkest hour that man ever lived, and all through sinful folly. With the sense of right and wrong, Thou, O God, canst forgive where poor, frail humanity shouts, Good enough for him! Merciful Father, be my strength in this hour, or I perish, and by my own hand, and the curse upon all such be upon me! Deliver me, O my God, or I perish!"

Immediately following the preceding extract, the Opium Eater finds scrawled the following words without date :—

"Starvation for six months! O God, give me of that bread 'of which if a man eat he shall never hunger.'"

If death, either by design or accident, had overtaken me at that time, these expressions would have been taken as indicating suicide, which, no doubt, was a thought often with me. It seems hard to comprehend at the present time, the state of despair under which the above was written, after a lapse of eleven years ; but it will be readily understood only by those familiar, and constantly coming in contact with, such sad cases, although the scenes of poverty and starvation are not always companion pictures.

The fall and early winter of 1883 found me in a desperate state. Not realizing on my gambling suits, I had been negotiating with a speculative young man and his lawyer, whereby in consideration of $1,000 spot cash, I was to relinquish my claim in full to them, having sadly realized the truth of the adage that "a bird in the hand is worth two in the bush," especially when your gunning is to be done with lawyers. The negotiations, however, did not materialize.

Death was a thing much to be desired, and the spirit of

suicide was my daily companion. I had no fears now, such as actuated me when I sought freedom in the hospital, that I might puncture an artery and die. Hope had forever fled in this direction, and I knew of, and expected, no release except in death. If it is

> Man's inhumanity to man
> Makes countless thousands mourn,"

it is man's humanity to man that has, and will, make countless millions rejoice. The Opium Eater found an occasional oasis in this desert of life. They are as refreshing to think of and dwell upon as are those real sources of life to the traveler through the hot and burning Sahara. Hope almost gone, he suddenly comes upon the refreshing desire of his life — water. In my extremity I am indebted to no special race or color ; religious and irreligious alike afforded relief and succor in dire necessity.

I recall an incident here corroborative of how circumstances and surroundings have, and probably ever will have, a great bearing upon the treatment we receive at the hands of our fellows. While sleighing with an acquaintance who was very much under the influence of liquor, and who was driving carelessly and recklessly, and at the same time endeavoring to show the Opium Eater the fine "points" of his colt, we came suddenly to grief. Driving too far up on the banking made by the snow's being thrown from the sidewalk, our sleigh capsized, just in time for me, being on the left of the sleigh, to fall under the forefeet of a horse attached to an approaching sled. My friend being larger, and on the right hand side, and having the reins, pitched forward in such a manner as to come in contact with the hind feet of the horse, and the sled

passed over him. When he was taken up, to all appearances he was lifeless. His scalp hung detached and lacer-
ated over his right ear, and he presented a ghastly sight
as he lay limp upon the white and frozen snowbank. He
was taken to the police station, and I looked about for a
surgeon. His services were not required, however; another, being nearer at hand, was rendering what assistance
was necessary. The accident had completely "unstrung"
the Opium Eater. I was without either my morphine or
syringe, and I felt that I wanted them badly.

"Doctor," I said, retiring with him to his office, after
seeing my friend attended to, "I would like the loan of
your hypodermic syringe for a few moments. I have not
mine with me." He readily granted my request, and in his
presence I injected a full "hypo" of morphine — thirty
drops—into my arm. He looked at me with astonishment
pictured on his countenance, but saw that I was familiar
with my work, my well-pitted arm bearing witness. For
the accommodation, and trouble incident to the accident, I
gave him the professional fee.

A year or two after this incident, under circumstances
as remote as the east is from the west, the Opium Eater
had occasion to call upon a physician under far more distressful conditions, if possible. It happened in this wise :
The needle of a hypodermic syringe is no larger than an
ordinary sewing needle. If I may use the expression, it is
"drilled" through, and the passage is, of course, necessarily, exceedingly fine. A gold wire rod, almost like one of
the hairs of your head in size and fineness, is supposed to
be kept in this needle after use, so that it may be kept
clear. Morphine easily congeals or dries, leaving a hard

substance in the needle, which becomes a barrier to the flow of this "elixir of life"; and this usually happens to the habitué at critical times and unseasonable hours if the golden ramrod is left out of it for protection. It has happened hundreds of times to me, but at no time so inconvenient as on this occasion.

It was early one Sunday morning that I awoke—as only advanced opium eaters awake, with only one thought, and that for morphine—and found it necessary to take some of the stimulant, but the avenue through the needle was blocked. My gold wires were old and bent; and had been discarded, and negligently I had failed to procure others. The old ones were brought again into requisition. My nerves were in a better condition to handle a crowbar than a slender, delicate affair like this, and to guide and drill out this great boulder in a needle's trunk! I worked and labored on for more than two hours, with that patience and perseverance known only to those working for the accomplishment of a purpose, drinking some of the bitter drug to compose me. Years of experience had made me quite proficient in overcoming this and other obstacles, and necessity had revealed to me many methods of removing this blockade. But now they all failed. I was in despair. I had drank more than half of my morphia,—a most profligate waste,—and with only a small return in feeling for the amount squandered. It was too precious stuff to be so recklessly wasted. At last I stole out of my barren and cheerless room. Of a physician whom I knew by meeting almost every day, and who had a kindly countenance, I determined to ask the loan of a needle for a moment. I could have purchased one for seventy-five cents or a dollar.

But that was "big money" at that particular time. I went to the doctor's house, and calmly and briefly, but earnestly, I presume, related my predicament, and asked for this trifling and insignificant loan. I did not get it.

Leaving the doctor's residence, I entered a large drug store and asked to look at some "hypos," actuated by the thought that perhaps I might purloin one. Delusive hope! But if my memory serves me aright, the clerk gave me, or I abstracted, one of the wire rods, and returning to my room I resumed my labor of drilling the mountain of obstruction, in the shape of a tiny clot of congealed poison, that stood between me and my immediate heaven. My efforts were finally crowned with success, and the joy experienced was far greater than those not similarly situated can appreciate if words could express it.

How unlike the physician who had unhesitatingly not only loaned me the use of his "hypo," but his morphine, when my tipsy friend met with the accident and my shattered nerves required a powerful sedative. The reason is obvious: On the one hand money and respectability; on the other a seeming lack of both.

How different, too, on scores of occasions under like circumstances, an employee in one of Boston's largest surgical instrument-making establishments, divining my needs, and knowing full well my poverty, loaned me needle and "hypo," and gave me credit where reimbursement looked hopeless. He, too, has since joined the hosts invisible.

May his soul find sweet repose!

CHAPTER XII.

I BELIEVE IN GOD AND CHRIST, BUT HAVE NO RELIGION.

ALL MEN believe in a Supreme Being,—in what
we call God. The Opium Eater was surely no
exception to the rule. We have a Book which
the Christian world reveres, and calls holy, because they
believe it contains a revelation of God to man, and more
particularly from the fact that in Jesus Christ was manifested the character and love of God toward mankind.
The Word of God is distinguished by much that is called
miraculous or supernatural, and is not believed by a large
class of humanity today on the one hand, and is believed
by a large body of mankind on the other. The greater
portion of the latter class belong to the so-called "Visible
Church," embracing, as it does, a large number of religious
sects or creeds. These manifestations, however, by this
Supreme Being were simply to establish a form of religious
worship in the centuries long past; and in this age of
enlightened intelligence, and wisdom, and learning, this
Word of God is a revelation confirmatory in itself sufficient to convince all for all coming time that the wonderful events narrated therein, and those especially that clus-
ter around the Standard-bearer whom God sent into the
world to proclaim Truth and show salvation, ended the
visible supernatural manifestations, and that they will
never occur again, is the generally accepted interpretation.

In order, therefore, that the partial caption of this

work, "From Bondage to Freedom," may be established, the Opium Eater incorporates in the following pages the incidents leading to a culmination and a realization of this condition,— freedom!   However, that which follows is not written at the instigation of any man or set of men ; is not in the interest of any church or sect or religious body of worshippers, nor for the propagation of any religious proselytes.   If I represent none, I cannot, therefore, misrepresent any.   I give the reader this information that he may not lay aside the further perusal of these "Confessions," from the fact of the character of Truth that they may henceforth contain of Divine interposition, should he have such misgivings.   Prevention from the opium habit and kindred vices have, however, largely actuated me in these recitals.

The reader will have gathered sufficient from my early life experiences to show that the Opium Eater was not what may be termed "religiously inclined,"— taking the generally accepted meaning of the word "religiously" to indicate one who loved to attend religious worship, to be present at the family devotions, to be found at the Sunday school, and a reader of the Bible.   I loved the sincerity of my mother's religious faith,— her prayers at our bedside, her example and teaching, her knowledge, confidence, and love of God, without any of the sham piety of desiring to be known as a Christian in name, but rather by deeds of love and acts of kindness.   I never have been a scoffer at any one's religious convictions, however absurd they might seem to me.   If they believed them, and were happy in them, why should I ridicule what I could not controvert?   Hence the reader will see that the re-

ligious side of my life had very little in common with
the religious traditions of the ages. I was a stranger to
the Church, to its customs, and its forms. I do not
purpose here to take issue with any on religious grounds.
We all cherish our opinions, but they are ever subject to
changes,— and radical ones, at times, as the history of
human events clearly shows, and will continue to show
until man shall be no more and time shall end. But to say
that in these dark and direful times of poverty and wretchedness I did not even meditate on things pertaining to
the future, would not be stating the truth. My misery
was complete; my physical sufferings at times simply
agonizing. I did not even reveal my destitute circumstances to my brothers, at a distance; feeling myself to be
the guilty cause of all my distress, I tried to fight it out
silently and alone. Then, too, the treachery and villain-
ous conduct of my lawyers and others in money matters,
had tended rather to make me desperate, and man and his
promises were like broken reeds. God, of course, was an
unknown and an unthought of source of deliverance; yet
to the soul thus cut off from human sympathy, there was
always hope in His mercy. My thoughts often turned in
this direction.

Who could give me more consolation and hope than one
who in sorrow and deep afflictions and vicissitudes of life
had sought and found that "peace which the world cannot
give nor take away,"— my mother. Her letters in those
dark days were living epistles of hope and light, and it
would afford the Opium Eater great pleasure to incorpo-
rate many of these heaven-sent messages of a Christian
mother's never-dying love for her wayward and prodigal

son, if space and the object of these writings permitted. Those to be found inserted in chapters following will bear witness to the love and constancy of true motherhood.

Had my situation in life been like many of those whose confirmed use of opium has come down to us, surrounded as they were by external comforts and home enjoyments, I could and probably would have plodded on, finding temporary relief in various poisons and anæsthetics, and in looking for the King of Terrors to give a happy release in a much-desired end of my misspent life and worthless existence.

On the twenty-third day of January, 1883, in the early evening hour, seated in a saloon in Boston Highlands, where the Opium Eater had passed much time for several months, my brother entered, and called for and drank a glass of liquor. I was not included in the "call." Small things often worry us most. I felt this slight keenly. My purse had always been his. His money was hard-earned, and with small wages, at that. I said nothing, but I thought, and to some purpose, as time has since demonstrated. I had then been sixty-four hours without food, and months, I may truthfully add, with little that might be called such. Having tossed off his liquid refreshment, he handed me a letter, — a letter from my mother,—and left the place.

CHAPTER XIII.

I FIND A FRIEND AND EMPLOYMENT.

TO RESUME. The Opium Eater put the letter handed him by his brother unread into his pocket. My mother's letters — as extracts taken from a large package and incorporated in this volume bear witness — always had much to say about the never-ending theme of Christ's love for sinners. It was not the love invisible, however, that I felt so much in need of just at that time, as that love made manifest in substantial and material things to a starving man. I did not then know the connecting link between the two.

It was a bitter cold night. I got up from the table at which I was sitting and walked out of the barroom into the dark and cheerless night, not knowing what to do or whither to go. As I went along I recalled having seen a sign giving notice of a meeting in one of the more cosmopolitan churches in the neighborhood; and thither I bent my footsteps, seeking only shelter from the cold and inclement weather.

The meeting was too soon over, for it again drove the Opium Eater forth into the pitiless night. Passing out, I was accosted by a young man, who asked me one of those commonplace questions one often hears at revival meetings, "Are you on the Lord's side?"

There was a savageness in my heart, whetted by hunger, but without intending rudeness or incivility, or even with the thought of suggesting assistance, I replied,—

"Feed my body before you feed my soul."

"Isn't your name Cole?" he asked.

"It was once," I answered.

"I used to see you quite often," he said, naming the place and the surroundings of better and more prosperous days. He asked me the meaning of the expression about "feeding the body," and I told him of my hunger. He asked many questions in regard to myself, occupation and habits, and before leaving me called into a store and made a purchase of some crackers and cheese, and when on the street presented them to me. The act was genuinely a Christian one, and for which I was very thankful. In parting with him he exacted a promise from me that I call on him at his place of business the next day.

The Opium Eater returned to his cold and comfortless shelter and made, at least, a thankful repast.

In keeping with my promise, the next day I called on my new-found friend, and we went over my life, and I confided to him my opium habit, in connection with my use of alcoholic stimulants. He asked me if I could work. I told him that I would gladly make the effort if an opportunity were afforded me. "Would you sign a pledge of total abstinence from intoxicating liquors?" he inquired; and assuring him that I would, he produced a New Testament with a pledge form pasted on the inside of the front cover, and after erasing and making the pledge conform to alcoholic beverages alone, the Opium Eater signed it.

I reproduce the form of the pledge here, which is one

well known in the North End Bethel Total Abstinence
Society of Boston, who have enrolled upon a large scroll
some thirty-three thousand signers, and known particularly
in this locality as the Mariner's Exchange.   Eleven years
from the signing of this pledge the Opium Eater spoke
from its platform, and read the pledge from the Testament
signed by him.   It is, perhaps, useless to add that that vow
has not been violated "up to date."   It reads as follows :—

BOSTON, Jan. 24, 1883.

THIS NEW TESTAMENT is received as a memorial of a
solemn pledge by me, Henry G. Cole, that I will
not taste of intoxicating beverages from this glad
hour even to the close of life's short voyage.   May the
author of this holy book (who has declared in 1 Cor. 6 : 10,
no "drunkard shall inherit the kingdom of God") give
me strength to keep this pledge inviolate.

[My friend's name witnessed it.]

The Opium Eater's physical condition was deplorable—
emaciated and wrecked.   With an exceptional short inter-
val, here and there, I had been a stranger to employment
for more than three years.   The low rate of wages meted
out to unfortunates had more than once been withheld,
and often the opportunity of earning them was denied
me.   Then, too, if it were possible, the opium habit is
more demoralizing in crushing out ambition for honest toil
than that of alcoholism.

The hope of ultimately receiving some of the money
won by my counsel in the gambling suits had kept the fires
of life still burning, and buoyed me up with the thought,
De Quincy like, that with some of this wealth the Opium
Eater would purchase, and retire to, the remote, isolated,

and wild farm among the New Hampshire hills, before spoken of,— and, unknown and forgotten, eke out his few remaining months or years beyond the reach or contact of human beings, except those who would be actuated to share my lot by the hope of remuneration in the property he should leave. The world contained but one thing of importance to me — morphine. Hope of heaven — there was none. Hell and despair I was already in. Death was the oblivion in which I desired to find the eternal resting-place !

That abandoned farm among the barren hills, where a few straggling sheep grazed the thin, dry grass, the deep receding valley, and in the distance the horizon kissing the bosom of a calm lake, was in harmony with the Opium Eater's wretched hope, whence from out the portals of this forsaken tabernacle of man, the messenger of another world would bear his spirit hence to the waiting ferryman !

In Alexander Selkirk's ode to " Solitude," he makes life unbearable to the one who made a choice of being put on the lonely island of Juan Fernandes ; but provided the Opium Eater could have had such a choice, and been surrounded with his favorite drug, such a haven would have filled completely his heart's desire. He feels confident that no melancholy strain like this would have been his :—

> " O Solitude ! where are the charms
> That sages have seen in thy face ?
> Better dwell in the midst of alarms,
> Than reign in this horrible place !"

How foolish seems that dream tonight which was once so golden ! Situated far from neighbors, and miles yet from civilization, it would have required a drug store and a surgical-instrument establishment within my domicile to have kept my mind at ease.   But such was the "dream of despair" that made life bright in those dark days, to which I now look back in horror.   Death,—a thousand deaths to such a life!

But now I must think of work.   And gladly would I do my best, I told my friend, if one could be found who would give me employment.   He had already spoken to the superintendent of the printing department of a nationally known periodical with regard to employing me.   I had an interview with this man, and withheld nothing in regard to my life and condition.   He surveyed me critically, said he would give me employment, but as ladies were employed in the office, my appearance would debar me from work unless I could get more presentable clothing.

My friend, to whom I communicated the facts, not thinking of this obstacle of debarment, wrote a note to the missionary in charge of affairs at the church before mentioned.   He asked me to deliver it on my way to my room. The result was that the gentleman addressed in the note, invited me into a room connected with the church and clothed me from head to foot in cast-off garments, gave me some advice, offered a prayer, handed me a dollar, and expressed the hope that the Opium Eater would not get drunk and pawn the clothes.

The following day or two I went to work.

The abandonment of liquor and of living a more decent and respectable life, began to manifest itself.   I began to feel like a different creature.   A new spirit seemed to have taken possession of my being.   My work proved more than satisfactory, if I was not misinformed by outside parties. I lived more than half moral, and far in advance of my expectations. I found no advisers or spiritual counsellors. My friend often spoke of a cêrtain "Reverend" who "would put me on my feet" — whatever that meant — "when he returned from his absence." But on his return, he was not unlike the priest and the Levite on Jericho's highway,— who passed by on the other side. It was just as well, however.

My daily injection of opium did not increase in volume, nor did I experience the terrible agony caused by the tenderness and sensitiveness of the flesh, that I had experienced when living without the comforts of food and decent shelter. However, it was by no means a pleasant or agreeable task. So hardened does the flesh become by morphia thus used, that the glass barrel of this instrument is often forced from its connection with its metallic ends. Often have I been obliged to "solder" it together, then, by using every expedient known to the opium taker, find a place on the human form where the flesh seemed more soft and pliable, that the drug might find easy absorption ; and at other times the drug would be forced back over the packing of the syringe, so dry and unyielding had become the flesh.

During the next few months, without coming in contact with any spiritually minded adviser, except my mother by letter, and making no claim or pretension to anything like Christian character, the Opium Eater had aspirations and hopes inspired, if for nothing higher than a loathing and contempt for the vices and sins he had been familiar with and indulged in so excessively for years.

My mother's letters,— and, far more, her example,—

were living epistles to me. Every break from a standard set up by me caused me remorse. My habits of morphine and tobacco were never-ending sources of misery, and I longed to be free from the latter, if I had no hope of release from the former.

As I look back through a vista of eleven years removed from the scenes which I am describing, the life I lived was not unlike that of many professing Christians; yet there was very little Christianity about it. With the necessities of a common existence provided for, I felt more than thankful to a power that I recognized as that of God. But real transgressions of God's law did not bring that remorse of conscience and sincere repentance that sin of any kind or description ought to bring. My ideal had not been set on a living Christ. My bondage forever precluded such an example. I went to a cosmopolitan church and attended Sunday school, but my mind was not strengthened, or my life encouraged, by the vague speculations and theories advanced. Still, the influence was vastly different from the experiences of the past, though I walked alone.

The winter months passed, and the early spring found me improved in health, yet a skeleton in my emaciated looks. My brother would often give me some stinging cuts at my religious endeavors, when, in fact, I had made no pretension in that exemplary walk of life. I had simply forsaken the coarser trend of my life,— drink, and the barrooms, and the gambling house as a mode of gambling; but a lottery ticket and a game of "short" cards for small stakes with my brother was not an unusual incident, and brought no thought of wrong-doing,— not having, as I have stated, experienced deep spiritual emotions, and the nature of my bondage raising the barrier between me and my conceptions of righteousness. I looked upon the opium habit as a gross sin, and one which must, so long as indulged in, separate me from God. What, then, with this insurmountable barrier of opium, would the indulgence of a few minor weaknesses, long accustomed by years of complete abandonment thereto, amount to so long as I could not attain the desire of my heart? Why enumerate them? They were simply the curtailment of profligacies conservatively, and more wisely, and judiciously indulged in,— if sin can be conservatively and judiciously indulged in,— which, of course, it cannot be.

But my mind, however, was gradually being prepared for better things, and a change was going on impreceptible to me; but going on, nevertheless. The drink habit, strange to relate, never presented itself, and I do not now recall during those months, without any strong antipathy against it, one temptation in that direction, whereas for many years I had looked upon it as a necessity.

I often met old acquaintances to whom, on an invitation to "take something," I imparted the information that I had quit rum I hoped forever, and was always met with a kindly spirit. With fifteen years' association with men engaged in the liquor traffic, I do not recall treatment in a single instance other than that which one might look for and expect at the hands of any tradesman. That the saloon has often sheltered me from extreme cold, and afforded me sustenance in pinching hunger, I must truthfully admit. No class of men, however, can so faithfully portray the infamy of their business as the saloon keepers themselves.

CHAPTER XIV.

GLEANINGS FROM MY MOTHER'S LETTERS.

MAKING mention of my mother's letters, the Opium Eater makes selections from several received about this time, which were taken from a large package. They speak for themselves.

C*** E********, Nov. 6, 1882.

My Dear Son:—

I do not know how to thank you enough for your kind letter, which did me so much good, and I am so glad that I have not offended you in any way ; nothing could be further from my intentions than to wound any one's feelings, much less my own children, whom I long to bless. My heart is bound up in them, and their tribulations are more painful to bear than my own.

Dear Henry, you say that the passion for gambling has died out. God grant that it may be so, and hard, painful, and severe as your experience has been, it will be cheap enough if you are victorious over the foe.

My heart bounds with joy and gratitude at the wish you express to be a Christian. My dear son, "your fate is in your own hands ;" it is yours to determine the way in which you shall go. Nothing is more conspicuous in Christ's teachings than the confidence he places in man's ability to choose the better part, however far he may have strayed, and none knew better than he how hard it is for a man to enter the kingdom of heaven ; but none the less did he enjoin men to "seek first the kingdom of God," and He accepts the first faint indications of a better will. He pities and forgives the penitent, and extends to them His hand, that they may walk with trembling, faltering steps in the ways of holiness. How I wish that I could help and strengthen you. No words can express the joy and gratitude that would fill my heart to know that you were a true Christian ; night and day I pray for each one of you.

I am reading a volume of sermons which I so wish you could read. They are written by Scotch divines, whose theology is of the progressive and modern type, and dedicated to Dean Stanley. I think they would be so helpful to you.

I wish with all my heart you could get into a hospital, if it would cure you of the opium habit ; but if you cannot, is there not some mode of treatment you could make use of ? None but God knows how grateful I was to hear of Willie's (my brother) having such a respectable situation, and just what I was praying that he might get. I have been trying ever since to be a better Christian for God's goodness to him.

Your ever affectionate mother.

C*** E********, Dec. 24, 1882.

DEAR HENRY :—

No words can convey how welcome your letter was to me ; it needed no addition of money to awaken in me the most rapturous gratitude to God that I have experienced. For three days and nights I had suffered so intensely from suspense, that I could only hope and pray that God would give me that rest from sorrow which only death can bring, but that morning before your letter came I tried humbly and earnestly to bow in submission. The Saviour gave me the gracious words of comfort, "Fear not; only believe." And when your letter came, notwithstanding poor Willie's illness, it seemed the most gracious benediction that was ever bestowed upon me; and though I am feeling quite miserable in health, I am so thankful I do not care about it. I only wish I could add poor W.'s cough and weariness to my own, and give him health and strength again. . . . . Have you no fear, should you get the money [from my gambling cases], that you would be tempted to gamble again? Strong passions do not die easily. Don't trust in your own strength, but look to Him who is "able to keep you from falling."

Dear Henry, you say that you pray to God for His Spirit (what but His Spirit gives you such a desire?). But you seem to think He does not hear you. That reminds me so much of "Robert Falconer," that I have turned to the book. It says: "Robert had not the vaguest idea that God was with him; but looking back to the time when it seemed he cried and was not heard, he saw that God had been hearing,— had been answering all the time." You must be obedient to His voice, and looking to him for help, strength, and guidance, must forsake sin and do his will. You are right in believing that the sin you allude to [opium taking] stands between you and God; and do not be offended with me, my dear son, when I add that a life of usefulness only can be acceptable to him. True penitence consists in forsaking sin, and bringing forth "works meet for repentance." As to the unpardonable sin, the only proof a person has committed it, is their entire insensibility to the subject. No sin that a person is penitent for, and willing to forsake, can be unpardonable, for this is the very condition in which God can bless them. "For that the Lord came. For that God lives, and loves like the most loving man or woman on earth,—only infinitely more so." Now, can you not believe that God loves you, and desires above all things that you shall be victorious over sin? Now, my dear son, cherish this blessed influence by a loving obedience. How I long to strengthen and help you! . . . . .

P. S.—Please write very soon again, and let me know how W. is, and how your soul prospers. Most earnestly shall I pray for you both. With much love,

Your ever affectionate mother.

——

C*** E*********, April 30, 1883.

My Dear Son :—

Your kind letter was received last evening, and I was very grateful to hear from you. I had been feeling much cast down with regard to you and Willie, and find that, as usual, I have an intuitive perception — or a prophetic spirit — in matters that concern those I love.

I have realized that the weather, with its chilly, piercing winds, must be extremely unfavorable to Willie's condition, and wonder that he is able to keep up at all. What a relief it would be to me if I could care for him as I did in childhood.

You also express discouragement, physically and spiritually, and seem to feel that the privilege of earning your

living is denied you.   My sympathies are warmly excited,
and I long to cheer, and be helpful to you.   Of course
such a condition of things must sadden me ; but what was
ever gained by despondency?   Is it not the devil's own
weapon to benumb and paralyze the soul ?   His motto is :
"It is of no use; our sins and weaknesses are so great
that we can neither hope nor expect to get rid of them.
He is willing that we should be saints tomorrow, provided
we keep on sinning today."   But the Gospel says we are
saved by hope.   "Courage, hope, and faith make so large
a part of goodness, that Christ aims chiefly to encourage
us."   He says that he came "not to call the righteous,
but sinners to repentance"; that he will not "break the
bruised reed, nor quench the smoking flax."   I know of
no symbols more utterly expressive of weakness than
these, and many times in hours of discouragement they
have comforted me.   Our very sins and weaknesses are
the pledge of the Saviour's helpfulness,— the only require-
ment being to feel our need of Him.   How grateful I am
that your conscience is so quickened, and that sin is growing so hateful to you.   How can you interpret it other
than the Holy Spirit striving in your heart ?

Dear Henry, would it not be possible to give up the
use of opium at once ?   I am ignorant of the effect of
such a course physically ; but oh ! it seems to me that it
would be better to suffer the tortures of the damned awhile
in this world, and violently take the kingdom of God by
force, than to feel as you now do,— that you are not doing
God's will, and that Christ does not accept you.   What
other barrier can there be than this, when His gracious
words are so full of encouragement : "Whosoever cometh

unto me, I will in no wise cast out"? It seems to me that if you could only cast out this devil in Christ's name, your course would be upward and onward. Most earnestly will I entreat that you may have strength to overcome ; for the only test of Christ-life in the soul is doing his will.

I should be grateful to have you send me Mr. Beecher's Friday evening lectures. I do not have the "Christian Union"; it was a great help to me spiritually. I am reading sermons by Rev. James Freeman Clarke. They are entitled, "Go Up Higher ; or, Religion in Common Life." They are so practical that I wish you would get them to read ; they might be very helpful to you. . . . . Dear Henry, I thank you for thinking of my troubles and trials. Yes, notwithstanding many blessings and mercies, I am sometimes sorely tried. Many thanks are due you for all the kindness you have shown me ; and if you feel that you were at all lacking in consideration of my welfare, you may rest assured that you are more than forgiven ; that the greatest blessing that you can confer upon me is to take a noble stand for Christ. Accept a mother's warmest love and blessing.

The careful reader will have noted that two of the dates to my mother's letters were in close proximity to that of my despairing prayer of Oct. 25, 1882. Such, too, is the subtle power of opium that, under its influence, rags are transformed to purple and fine linen ; the soul, famishing with hunger, rises from its spell as though satiated with good things ; and the barren and fireless abode is changed to one of comfort and genial glow. Such were the conditions under which the Opium Eater wrote to bring forth the royal messages of love from his mother.

I ATTEND REVIVAL MEETINGS, AND MEET A DISSEMBLER.

CHAPTER XV.

EARLY in the spring I had been invited to attend a meeting where, I was informed, I would hear the experiences of men who had reformed under the revival influence of Moody and Sankey. I went to the meeting in great expectancy, but was more than disappointed with its results. Two men only spoke of their having been reclaimed, and one of these had no madder disorder than infidelity ; the other's talk I passed by as not containing much that would encourage me, and which I might define more properly by quoting the utterances of the Saviour as recorded in Matthew 23 : 10.

I attended a meeting similar in character, held at the same church, on another occasion, and, with my head bowed in my hand, I was startled somewhat to hear a man relate an experience that inspired me with deep interest. On looking up, I thought I recognized in the speaker a face familiar to me in my gambling-house days ; and to make myself doubly sure that I could not be mistaken, at the close of the meeting I inquired of an elderly lady, who manifested an interest in the Opium Eater by speaking to him about the welfare of his soul, the name of the public confessor, and found that he bore the same name as that of my gambling-house acquaintance.

Of course my curiosity was aroused. Interested, I went again, in the hope that circumstances might bring me in contact with him, and from his own lips I would get the truth. I was a skeptical Thomas. Again I went and listened while he poured forth eloquence on the theme of his conversion, and he seemed to hold the undivided attention and have the respect of the audience. At a meeting on the Sunday evening following I found my opportunity. In a small room in the church there had been held what was termed a "redeemed men's" meeting, with a conspicuous absence, however, of reformed men. My gambling acquaintance was the "leader" of the gathering. At its close, while engaged in conversation with several ladies, he looked up, and seeing the Opium Eater standing a little distance away, he approached, together with the ladies. Extending his hand, he opened the conversation with,—

"Where have I seen you before?"

I gave him a significant look, intending to convey to him the thought that I did not care to relate just where I saw him last in the outer world; that if he had a "good thing," I did not desire to destroy it by a public proclamation. Alas, such is the skepticism of our dwarfed human natures!

However, as he still seemingly desired the knowledge, I imparted it thus :—

"Well, sir, the last time I saw you, you was in 12 Montgomery Place (a fashionable gambling house in those days). You called the 'turn' for fifty dollars — king-duce — and won. I played against you."

"Ah, yes," he acknowledged. And turning to the ladies, he remarked, "You see how my past life haunts me!"

They passed on and out, and I then asked him with regard to what I have stated. He told me a remarkable story, which I then believed, and expressing the desire to pray with me, I granted the request.

His story, in brief was, that having bankrupted health and fortune at gambling and dissipation, and driven to despair, he had resolved on self-destruction. To this end he had procured the services of a hackman to drive him to the wharf where he was to end things mortal by drowning himself. But the voice of conscience called him to himself, and he had the horses' heads changed in the direction of a clergyman's house, who, pointing out the better way and praying with him, he had been saved. Of course the thought of using one's reasoning faculties seemed to be swallowed up in simple belief, and why should the hopeless Opium Eater question the veracity of the testimony, in his weakened mental and physical condition?

However true his statements may have been, this I do know, that like the sow that was washed, he again returned to his wallowing in the mire, but not before he had succeeded in gathering in a goodly amount of " revenue " from those who who did not possess the wisdom of the worldly. He was a hypocrite. Nevertheless, his testimony had sufficient weight to draw me there again, and with the following results.

CHAPTER XVI.

MY BLESSED EMANCIPATION FROM MORPHIA.

ON MAY 7, 1883, the Opium Eater again went to the services being held in the aforesaid church. I did not hear anything during the meeting that particularly impressed itself upon me, and at its close I lingered a moment to allow the more hurried ones to pass out ; and as I followed in the rear, and approached the door, I heard a voice — sweet, musical, and pure. Raising my eyes to see from whence so heavenly a sound proceeded, they beheld the loveliest face they had ever looked upon, with a small, beautifully shaped hand extended toward me, and the welcome sound of "Brother," as she took my emaciated hand in hers. She was attired in deep mourning, and at her side stood another, similarly dressed, older, but not less noble, a sister. The scene was a strange one, and the interest manifested by the younger, who did all the talking, in a soft, inspired, musical tone of voice, with an earnest truthfulness, riveted me to the spot.

I shall relate further on the incidents that led up to this remarkable, and to many it may seem strange, interview.

If the reader shall have discovered any merit in this feeble record of a rescued life, I can unhesitatingly say that the experience of this young woman furnishes one unparalleled in spiritual power, and singularly beautiful in its purity, innocence and exceeding interest. I listened in deep silence to her story of Divine interposition, and the emotion that filled me at its close found vent in an "open confession" of my life as a degraded sinner past hope, and an opium eater.

I could conceive how God could love a pure and spotless woman, innocent and confiding as a child; but for a man, and a sinner like myself, the case was far different. I mentioned to her these doubts in my wretched existence, and closed by saying,—

"I am addicted to the use of morphia; God never can do anything for me."

Why do tears flow unbidden from the eye, and speech become inaudible and the voice beyond control on such occasions? As I parted with this angel of light, her hand was again given to me with an accompanying word of encouragement. In attempting to pass a group of religious people who evidently had been interested spectators to this uncommon scene,—as "Gertrude" was well known in the church as one "wonderfully raised up by the Lord," —a clergyman "laid hands" on me, and would have further detained me; but the same voice, now like "one having authority," bade him let me pass on.

Out into the cool air of that beautiful May night, my thoughts engrossed in the testimony I had just heard, I walked toward my room, situated more than a mile away. Alone, with characteristic habit, I put my hand into my pocket and brought forth my tobacco as an accompaniment to help my musings, and was about to take a piece of the favorite morsel, when my thoughts were turned on the uncleanliness of this habit in connection with what I had just heard, and I was forced by conviction to cast it away. Probably I never desired a "chew" more than I did then; but I threw it away, and I am impressed with the thought that the next morning I procured another piece.

In my room, tired and weary, and deeply perplexed, I knew not what to do. To leave off my morphine meant a death far more horrible than suicide.

The Opium Eater took his "hypo" and retired.

I had made a promise to the young woman that I would come to the meeting the next evening. A series of meetings were being conducted by a revivalist, who made the claim of having been reformed from drink and converted from infidelity. He did not, however, inspire any great expectations or hope in me, believing as I then did that the former habit could be fought and conquered by the individual himself, as I had then done for months past, without claiming reformation or help from God, though I now know I was being sustained by that invisible power. Infidels (unorthodox) there might be, but so far as a disbelief in a Supreme Intelligence, Power or Being are concerned, I did not believe that existed where ordinary intelligence dwelt.

When evening came I reluctantly wended my way toward the church. I found on entering, however, that the order of service had been changed, and instead of being in the vestry, as on the previous evening, the body of the church had been substituted. A little late, intentionally, I cautiously looked about for a place where the Opium Eater would be least likely of being observed, and the gallery being unoccupied, with but one exception, I passed in and took a seat directly behind its solitary occu-

pant. He was a man well nigh threescore and ten years.
In connection with the evangelist, the pastor of the
church occupied the pulpit. He is a clergyman of repute
in the Baptist denomination, and the author of various
works, among them being "The Ministry of Healing."
At the close of the short preaching or "exhorting" service, a most singular thing happened,— if we do not believe that intelligent forces exist about us. The clergyman stepped down from the pulpit, and ascending a short
flight of steps directly opposite, in a moment's time
was by the Opium Eater's side. He gazed intently and
earnestly for a moment at the emaciated form and sunken
countenance of the victim of folly and dissipation, like
one who looks with a pitying glance upon a picture wherein only misery and despair lingered, and out of which all
hope had fled. Speech failed him, so far as the Opium
Eater was concerned, but turning to the old gentleman, he
asked, in substance,—

"Are you on the Lord's side, brother?"

"For more than forty years," I heard the old man reply; and then, hesitatingly, the clergyman cast a look of
commiseration upon the Opium Eater, and passed down the
steps and from view.

Situated as I was, I could not see many of the audience
below, and, in general, they interested me very little. I
had not seen the "angel of light" who had ministered to
me the previous evening, and felt greatly relieved, than
otherwise. For how could I be saved? Perhaps she was
not there.

But I was mistaken. She had discovered my presence
from the first ; had witnessed all that had taken place from

"LIKE A CREATURE FROM THE WORLD CELESTIAL."—(*page 111.*)

the moment her pastor had left the sacred desk and abandoned his mission unaccomplished.

It was a trying moment to her. Powers known only to
those who have come in direct contact with them, strug-
gled for the mastery. Finally, raised from her seat by
power superhuman, she passed out of the main body of
the church into the vestibule and up the stairs and along
the length of the gallery of the church, as though borne
on "the wings of the wind," and like a creature from the
world celestial, she took a seat by my side.

What was said related to the surrender of my soul to
Him who had created it.

The evangelist was exhorting the unsaved, after the un-
scriptural methods of modern times, to accept the Saviour.
Of course, my companion urged me to comply with the
invitation. I lacked not only the courage of a public dec-
laration, but such an act on my part was freighted with
far greater consequences than any one could conceive,—
an abandonment of opium and an excruciating death, or a
worse fate in a drawn-out existence of imbecility.

Then, too, the presence of this beautiful and innocent
woman seemed to clearly manifest the gulf that separated
me from such a hope. I felt that her character might
suffer by lingering longer in my company, and when she
volunteered to accompany me down the steps, to lead my
faltering soul back to God, I refused the offer solely on
these grounds alone.

The old gentleman, however, who had been a willing or
unwilling listener,— perhaps both,— kindly proffered to
accompany me down to the altar. To this I assented, and
we went forward. The evangelist had also selected some

verse of Scripture,—to what end, the Opium Eater cannot say,—which the candidate was supposed to repeat
after him.   But I refrained from this catechising lesson, and instead, I solemnly asked God to have mercy
on my soul.   I pass over much that took place incident-
ally, and which was neither helpful nor inspiring, and at
the meeting's close, after a short conversation with my
deeply interested friend, I was glad of the opportunity to
take my departure.   And while she could have had no
knowledge of what an opium eater's life meant, she knew
by discernment that my terrible physical condition meant
more than suffering of an ordinary character.   Having
herself passed through the fiery ordeal of physical agony,
she knew the Power that could alone make my burden
light !

Did all of these occurrences of this part of the evening
happen by chance?   Did the Opium Eater, in his studied
endeavor to get in as secluded a place as possible, thwart
the leading of the Invisible?   How account for the act of
the clergyman?   He is not, I venture to remark, prone to
like acts.   Then, too, the solitary old man, and the part he
took.   To the young woman, of course, to many thoughtless minds, not so much attention will be paid.   Woman
is always doing deeds of goodness and mercy like this.
Did you ever note a face that was pinched by suffering
or by opium dissipation?   My facial expression beggared
description ; my general appearance was that of one in
extreme poverty.   Pity, you say, prompted her.   Nay, not
wholly.

The emaciated face, the garments I wore, the rings,
even, on my finger, were all familiar to her.   She had seen

that face — that ghastly, emaciated countenance — a long time before; not once, twice, but thrice it had been shown to her by One who alone makes revelations to whomsoever He will.   Hence her acts *are* accounted for.   [Not, however, till several years after the occurrences just narrated, when she had become the wife of the redeemed Opium Eater, did she confide these facts to him.]

But the acts of the others, myself included, were they governed and controlled by Him who takes cognizance even of the sparrows, and to whom all things are known and no mystery exists?

*   *   *   *   *   *

But now to my battlefield, where the final contest for freedom in death was to be fought.   It was a low-studded room, situated in the L part of the house, and very plainly and scantily furnished.

But to me, then, it was far more palatial and comfortable than any the Opium Eater had ever realized.   Appreciation of its meager comforts had taken the place of all desire for those fine adornments and luxuries of other days.   I entered that room as calm and tranquil in soul and spirit as an innocent man ascends the scaffold, or a heroic soul faces danger and eternity, with a confiding trust that the revealment beyond is not one to be shunned, but rather one that will far transcend the expectations of those who have lived in this hope of immortal life.   I thought on and carefully weighed the words of this young woman's testimony; an unmistakable revelation to me, and one full of hope, and not of fear.   The physical agony I felt prepared to undergo until released and set free by death.   I was, however, largely ignorant of the terrible manner in which opium or morphine users died under an entire abandonment of all narcotics, as the only case then familiar to me had passed away finally under the influence of sulphuric ether—the last agency to annihilate physical agony.   My past efforts in this direction were unthought of.   I realized that days must pass in untold distress, but finally, death —the welcome messenger of deliverance— would set me free !

The Opium Eater lay down upon an old lounge in the room, and thoughts passed panoramically across his vision. It seemed as though an invisible yet present voice aided him when he could not think fast enough concerning the individual cases of hypocrisy and inconsistencies that he had witnessed and been made a sufferer by in the lives of professing Christians.   And as a final argument to my now persuaded mind that it was all a mistake, words like these seemed to be rung in my ears by a voice clear as a bell : "There is nothing in it (God or Christianity).   People go to church to have a good time, the same as you go to the gaming-table, the theatre, the race-track and other places. That is their method of enjoyment ; this is yours."

Springing to my feet, I answered these concluding and convincing statements by an expression given vent to in words, as if I was really in the presence of a visible personage,—"That's so !"

Hardly had the words died from my lips, when a voice, quick, and sharp, and piercing, gave utterance to these words :   "This is your last opportunity !   If you go back on what you have done tonight,— this is your last chance !" As those words rang through my soul, there pervaded my being, from the crown of my head, a power that might be likened to a bolt of fire, and in its effect far more sedative than opium itself! I hesitated no longer. I determined to abandon morphia and all its kindred alliances. I made no agonizing prayer; I committed my soul to the love and tender mercies of a Supreme Being — my Heavenly Father. For the first time in years I disrobed and went to my bed without taking a "hypo" of morphine.

When I awoke it was morning, and I was a "new creation." My sleep had been as sweet and tranquil as that of a babe. No feeling or desire for the drug possessed me; no cold, nauseating sensations and symptoms manifested in the least decrease of the drug was apparent, or anxiety. I knew I was in the world, but I could hardly realize it. None of the signs and terrible agony described in this book accompanying the abandonment of opium were mine, in feeling or in look.

My brother occupied the room and bed with me. He did not know of the step I had taken, and I have no recollection of being awakened when he retired later, nor did I communicate it to one any else save the young woman to whom I have referred. What folly to have thought of finding sympathy from those who were unfamiliar with the habit, and what nonsense to have expected it from those who knew anything about it! The first class would have said it was a trifling affair; the latter, an impossible thing and useless to attempt. My brother, made familiar with it by a number of years of constant contact with myself, knew by observation the utter uselessness of trying to foil this demon by heroic resolution, by artifice, or by antidotes. When he first came to associate intimately with me, and occupy my apartments, he has told me that he had often stood beside my bed and watched intently for signs of life. My face under its deadly power would appear like marble, my arms often raised above my head, and not a muscle giving a perceptible evidence that the inanimate form contained life, the breathing being entirely undistinguishable, and for hours I would lie in this deathlike condition. He expected at any time to find me dead from over-indulgence.

So on that bright May morning he noted the change before I had recovered from my own cause for wonderment.

I was free! That I knew!

"What are you smiling at?" he asked, as he raised a bottle containing medicine to his lips, to take what is vulgarly termed a "smile."

"I am not smiling," I replied; and then I related to him the cause for the expression of happiness he had noted on my countenance. When I had finished, he looked earnestly and pleadingly toward me and said :—

"Hen (he always called me 'Hen'), you are not going to your work without taking your morphine with you, are you?"

I always carried in my pocket the case containing my "hypo" and a bottle of morphia. It was my life — my existence. He knew that. The last thing at night, on retiring, I would fill the syringe to the amount required and lay it within reach of my hand, in case I awoke in the night and felt in need of it, or to give me strength to rise by in the morning. I could forget everybody and everything, but not this. My brother had learned this by too many experiences; and fearful, no doubt, that I had lost my mind, or surely would, or that some calamity might come to me, he was forewarning me. Had he not asked the question, I should, without doubt, have taken it along with me.

"No," I replied; "I am done. I'm not going to take it any more."

He was one of those set and determined mortals himself, and without commenting further, he left the room and went to his employment.

Left alone, my joy was too great for utterance. I arose, but none of the feelings incident to the abandonment of this terrible habit manifested themselves,— no trembling, no weakness, no nausea, none of the symptoms described as following even the diminution of the drug were now apparent. A calmness supreme reigned within, and no thought or desire for the drug, that had been my waking demand for years, came into my mind.

An intense desire for food, a keen hunger, possessed me. A delicate eater at all times, my light appetite always had made it possible for me to obtain the best, and often in my destitute and wretched plight, my unwelcome presence forced its way into fashionable places of eating, as well as drinking, for this reason alone. More than once has the Opium Eater quietly been informed, by well-intentioned servants, at fashionable bars and hotels where in his profligate days he had been a welcomed guest, that his room would be preferable to his presence.

But this morning I felt an hungered, and as I entered the restaurant my first order to the waiter was that he immediately bring two cups of coffee. Coffee was a drink I had never used to any great extent; for years lager beer was indulged in at meals, as it counteracted some of the

injurious effects of morphine. But now, coffee, and two
cups at that, were always brought to me by the waiter as
soon as I entered. I followed this up but a short time,
and finally abandoned it altogether.

In flesh, too, I was frightfully emaciated. Morphine,
like liquor, acts differently on different constitutions.
Some persons grew stout and dropsical; others, like myself, thin, and emaciated, and bloodless. But now the
flesh seemed to fairly drop on to my bones, and I noted a
gain of many pounds in a comparatively short time.

As to my first day of emancipation : The reader has
been made familiar with the incidents of time in an opium
user's life. It never can be overdrawn. Language cannot
exaggerate it. But note the change. In more than forty
years of life I have never known so fleeting a day. We
all know many pleasures in life where Time has taken the
swiftest wings of flight. In a prodigal's life, perhaps, a
more infinite variety of such occasions may occur, but
none flee so swiftly as those where Love is the guest.
Love was the Opium Eater's guest that day ! The hours
passed as though Time had been obliterated. It was evening before I realized it. But to the outward observer I
presented a picture of one in physical distress. Through
my chest, and especially the small of the back and loins,
it seemed that a conspiracy existed for my overthrow. I
had to sit down quite frequently, for a moment, and then
I was up and at my work again. I do not now remember,
but probably I did not immediately confide to my associates what I had been taken from during the intervening
hours. My personal appearance had told its own tale of
life, except the opium part of it. I had made no confi-

dant of this to any one except the superintendent, when he gave me employment.

But when the noon hour came, I told those of my fellow-workmen who took interest enough in me to inquire the cause of my apparent physical uneasiness, the reason for for it, and my boundless gratitude to my Deliverer.

The feelings here described must not be confounded as bearing any relationship to those experienced by the Opium Eater in his attempts with antidotes and in his hospital struggle. Everything was clear and light; no disorder of the functions of the body, or excesses in any direction. I might liken the condition I have feebly attempted to describe as not unlike that experienced in an uncomfortably fitting shoe — a desire to get the foot out and give it rest; an expansion to make room for the crowded spirit that had taken possession of the soul!

When I arrived at my room at the end of my day's toil my brother had preceded me. He had passed a day of intense anxiety. He was prepared at any moment to hear of my being dead, or, worse — insane. Finding me all right he soon took his departure, leaving me alone to myself.

CHAPTER XVII.

ANOTHER CONFLICT WITH MY TEMPTER.

A S SOME little time intervened between the hour of the evening meeting at the church, I lay down on the lounge to rest. No thought or desire for morphine had entered my mind during the day, and I had not even "hankered" for my tobacco. While lying and contemplating with a grateful heart on God's goodness for my deliverance, and filled with that "peace which passeth understanding," I seemed suddenly to lose control of myself, or, rather, an impulse unprovoked by desire seized me, and I arose from my reclining position, and as calmly and collectedly as I have ever done anything in my life, I went deliberately to my bureau drawer, took out my "hypo" and morphine, and baring my left arm plunged the hypodermic needle under the skin, and had injected, perhaps, one half of the quantity of the morphine into it when, quick as a lightning flash, the power of God, made manifest as on the previous night, came upon me, and withdrawing the syringe I flung it from me.

The cuts on the following page represent hypodermic syringes for the subcutaneous injection of morphine by "opium eaters," and also enters largely into the treatment of inebriates in the so-called "gold cure" establishments.

The one in two pieces is a facsimile of its condition as I find it at this time, having picked it up in broken fragments from the floor and placed it in the case :—

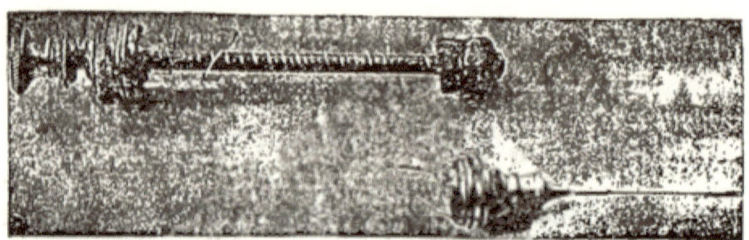

The Keeley graduate will need no introduction to this implement which, in the progress of his march to emancipation (?) from King Alcohol's thraldom, he is obliged to undergo at the rate of four "hypos" per day, until one hundred and twenty-four have been taken subcutaneously of the "most powerful poisons known in the Materia Medica," as it was tersely put by a "graduate," who spoke "with authority," before a meeting in the interest of the only genuine "gold cure":—

But the morphia that had entered my arm,— how about that ? I have before depicted the more than human sensation derived from an indulgence of this drug after but a few hours' deprivation from it beyond the allotted time for

its use. Will you believe me when I say, solemnly, before God, that the effect of the poison was as though it
had never been !   No sensation — no absorption, even ;
only a lump of raised flesh marked the unabsorbed drug !
Eleven years have since passed, and on that arm remains
to this day the most conspicuous mark of them all — this
one, taken under the circumstances described.

De Quincy and others tell us how, instantly, when the
opium victim is in need of his drug, the influence is felt,
and how quickly he is transformed from misery to peace ;
from torment indescribable to sensations heavenly.   My
mind and body were under a peace far more transcendent
than that ever derived from the highest distillation of the
poppy's famous nectar !

I went from this scene of conflict for a human soul to
the church.   When the opportunity offered, for the first
time in my life, in fear and trembling, I arose before a
large audience and related briefly the experiences of my
life and my deliverance from the bondage of an "opium
eater's" fate, by the manifestation of the power of God.

There was one, at least, besides myself in that large
throng who rejoiced with a joy unspeakable at the Opium
Eater's miraculous deliverance, and it was the one whose
deep interest in my welfare had caused her to plead before
her God my cause in supplication and tears all night long,
— Gertrude ; she whose testimony had been primarily the
cause in bringing about this glorious result.

The second night, like its predecessor, brought again to
me one of the greatest gifts of God to man,— sweet, un-
troubled sleep.   None of the symptoms incidental in the
abandonment of morphia made themselves manifest, and

in the morning I followed out the same course of dieting as on the previous day. The world indeed, and all things in it, had become new.

Before resuming my employment on the second day, I felt I was owing an explanation to my falsely self-styled Christian superintendent for my not working every moment on the day previous (excuse this plain reference to one, perhaps, of whom I ought to say nothing but kind words ; but truth demands it, and it is the truth). If his Satanic majesty controls anything, it is hypocritical humanity. "Clothed with a little brief authority," this man "made mountains out of mole-hills," and watched for every trifling opportunity to make his importance felt.

Meeting him, I briefly related my experience of the past few days, and asked the privilege of working, even without compensation, that my mind might be diverted as much as possible from myself and my physical condition. As has been stated, he had been made familiar with my morphine habit ; but instead of receiving encouragement from one professing so much piety in his Christian life, I was informed by him that he had noted my condition the day before, and had thought by the "bright light in my eyes" that I was going insane. I accounted to him for the light in my eyes on the ground that now for the first time in many years they looked forth soberly and unclouded by stimulants of any kind. And as for insanity, I expressed to him the thought that the Power that had released me did not intend any such sad fate should befall me.

After some further talk, pro and con, my superior in authority gave me the desired permission to work, but not a word of encouragement for the great battle before me did he utter. He went so far, even, as to forbid those of my associates who took a passing interest in me to inquire regarding my feelings ; and ordered them to attend to their own affairs, and those for which they were paid.

This day passed not unlike the first. Nature's laws transgressed were being assisted and supplanted by a supernatural or spiritual power. The battle was to be a sharp and fierce one, but I was free, so far as the desire or inclination for the drug was concerned. That was gone, root and branch, and the taste, even, no longer lingered in my mouth.

The morphine habit, like others,— tobacco, or alcoholism,— has certain characteristics accompanying it. It leaves a peculiar taste in the mouth, and an odor exudes from the body not unlike a mouldy, dusty, and sickening smell. It is the same with the indulgence of liquor to excess, or tobacco, only the odor is peculiar to the habit. In opium, however, this taste can be found at any time in the mouth by the process of suction, and particularly is this so when the demand for it is being pressed by the powers within or without, as you choose to attribute it.

CHAPTER XVIII.

MY FOE APPEARS IN ANOTHER FORM — SEVEN DAYS AND
NIGHTS WITHOUT SLEEP.

ON THE third night a different condition of things manifested themselves. Sleep fled. I found that I could not control myself in one position for any great length of time. I would roll myself up in the bed-clothing, and toss and twist around, and get into every conceivable position imaginable in order to find rest, but found none. My brother abandoned the room and moved into a spare chamber adjoining, and alone with the powers invisible I wrestled all night long.

No physical distress accompanied this restless and unceasing manifestation, such as pain; no illusions and distressful, agonizing pictures flooded the brain and made my existence a torment, as on former occasions when the least deprivation of the drug had been attempted, and innocent pictures upon the walls either had to be taken down or turned — the very objects portrayed becoming living realities and a source of unbearable annoyance.

My mind was as calm, and peaceful, and as resolute of victory, as though it had already been won; and there were no repinings, or regrets, or longings, or prayers that a different condition of things might exist! An intuitive knowledge seemed to possess me that all the weapons for a sure victory were within my grasp.

Little wonder at the heroic fortitude and calmness of

God's martyrs when sustained by such an overwhelming Presence! Little wonder, too, that the devotees of ignorance, bigotry and superstition trembled and fled before its calm and majestic sublimity!

Wonderful, too, was the speed of time! While I shifted my position constantly, no fascinating pleasure ever obliterated or moved the hands across Time's dial more swiftly than on that memorable night. I was fighting the battle with my invisible foe — the physical, the natural — with "the evidence of things not seen,"— the spiritual, the real weapon. And when it became time for me to arise, I went forth to my day's employment with no feelings of weakness or fatigue that I considered as a bar to the performance of an honest day of toil.

Then, too, I might portray these conflicting forces for a soul's mastery to have arranged an armistice, whereby the battlefield was to be my silent bedroom; for I recall having none of the marked symptoms of distress that I have described as occurring on the first day, when I sought an occasional rest from a standing position.

Night followed night, with little or no variation. Had I been as conversant, however, with this phase of life in an opium-taker's march to sheol as investigation and research have since made me, and that the "Appendix" to these pages will inform the reader, I might possibly have looked forward to my release in death when my strength failed; but unlike my former efforts and the experiences of others, my wonderful appetite and gain in strength and flesh precluded such a thought as death, to say nothing of the evidences of life that I had had in assurance.

I kept at my employment each day, and reported myself

at the church in the evening, in harmony with the written testimony here recorded. Whatever may have been its effect, I looked at the Church as the redemption office for lost and wandering souls among men, and I did not fully realize then how unaccountably strange my testimony of a living truth may have sounded : "Jesus Christ, the same yesterday, today, and tomorrow."

The fifth evening,— Saturday,— feeling desperately dis-spirited and alone, —there being no meeting, and with not a soul I felt at liberty to call on or see,— I shall never forget. The only one who extended a hearty and sincere invitation, was the last one I felt worthy of intruding my presence on — Gertrude.

The weather was mild, and I took a short walk and a fine bath, and felt greatly refreshed in body and spirit. In passing the door of a tobacconist, I was unconsciously entering it for my Sunday supply of cigars,— this being the first time since my redemption that this form of temptation had presented itself,— when I was suddenly called to myself by having the great High Priest of mankind presented to my mind with the "filthy weed" between his pure lips, and I passed meditatively along, the desire never having been gratified.

Returning to my room, and thinking over matters of the past few days, and wondering whether sleep would come to me, my mind reverted to my morphine. I got up, opened the drawer, and taking the bottle containing the solution of the drug, I emptied its contents out of the window. It was fortunate that I did so. This night was a repetition of the others, only more so. I rolled, and shifted positions constantly, but had no desire to walk about.   There was no eternity in the minutes, however, such as I before described, and which you will find corroborated in the experience of every opium taker who has ever had the courage to make one battle for freedom.

It was on this night, if my memory serves me rightly,— and it matters little if it does not,— that I lost faith, and for a short season I deeply regretted that I had been so hasty in throwing away all my morphia.   And as I tossed about without any knowledge of the time of night, I found on listening that when the clock in a church spire pealed out the hour, it was past the time when druggists, the last to seek their couches, had turned their lights low, pulled down their curtains, and retired, only to be aroused by calls of necessity.   Happy, indeed, was I when the Sabbath morning dawned with warm, refulgent sunlight, not only in the natural world, but also having its counterpart within my own soul.

Early on that beautiful Sunday morning I was up and out.   I walked down Shawmut avenue to Union Park, and had for a companion a tramp, who had "struck" me for a breakfast, which he got, together with a large slice of the Opium Eater's life, and an early edition of his redemption. Alas! who shall say that it was a case of pearls being cast at swine's feet!   In continuing my stroll, I entered a large saloon for my breakfast.   My appetite was better, then, so far as quantity was concerned, than ever in my life — before or since.   It was a nice place — that is, a first-class place to get a meal cooked to order.   I noticed that a sign hung across the large white sheet drawn over the shelves to obscure the fixtures back of the counter read— "Bar closed."   It was a lawfully licensed victualler-liquor saloon. I gave no thought to the bar or its contents, and while living a life of total abstinence I gave no heed to the sentimentalism that such a course precluded me from dining under a roof given up to this unholy traffic, but was patiently waiting for my order, when the waiter passed the "slip" I was sitting in to the adjoining one, in which were some men. He had on the tray a gin-cocktail and a glass of whiskey. I gave no thought to the matter until a few moments after his leaving it, when the aroma arising from the liquor came upon me with almost overpowering effect, and with a feeling of almost helplessness, I arose to my feet, and reeled out of the place like a drunken man. I felt dazed. I was mortified, and could not understand it. I saw the man behind the bar look with a stare of fixed astonishment, but I was powerless to even speak and explain my seemingly strange conduct. Possibly he may have thought that I had suddenly been taken ill. I never have returned to make an explanation ; nor did I repeat it again in a hurry. Years have passed, and to the strong yearnings of this subtle spirit I have not been a stranger, yet this man is the only mortal whose eyes have ever registered my discomfiture and retreat from King Alcohol.

There is but one class of individuals who can understand this — the confirmed drinking men or women who have made the attempt at reformation, and have passed through similar experiences. How often, alas, many fail to get through in their desperate battle against themselves !

However, it would be tedious to follow the moods and feelings in the succeeding days, but suffice it to say that I passed through seven days and nights without closing my eyes in forgetfulness, except once,— I think it was on the seventh from the abandonment of morphine, and the fifth without sleep,— when for a moment, it seemed, I closed my eyes and lost myself in apparent unconsciousness.

The bed I occupied was one of those old-fashioned, high-posted affairs. In this loss of myself, like one in dreams, I felt myself being hurled through space, when I was suddenly awakened by falling to the floor, and striking squarely on the top of my head. My brother came to my rescue, and I afterwards ascertained that the jar awoke the other occupants of the house. I was not at all hurt, and immediately got up, pugilistically speaking, before "time was called," and without assistance, smiling and feeling amused at the singular incident, but happy indeed to continue the conflict.

The tenth night, however, I slept a little,— an hour, I should judge,— and oh, how refreshing it was! Who can sing its praises after such a struggle! I gained on this a little each night, and in a short time I could sleep with the regularity of a child; and sleep has never deserted me from that happy hour to this, when I have not deserted it.

The foregoing may seem strange, untruthfully strange. Some one has said, "Honesty, of all things, is the most deceitful; the reason for it is because we have all been deceived." If any one desires to spend time in reading the testimony that can be adduced, they will find sufficient evidence to show that I am in harmony with others' experience so far as inability to sleep is concerned; and that confirmed opium users in forsaking opiates pass anywhere from a dozen to forty or more days without sleep!

Let him who thinks there is no divinity in this, beware!

CHAPTER XIX.

OTHER EXTRACTS FROM MY MOTHER'S LETTERS.

I INSERT this portion of a letter, without date, more from the fact of the reference made in it to Dr. Lowell, and his opinion of the condition of the opium-taker's will power, and from its tenor I am led to believe that it must have been written after my deliverance.

"Dr. Lowell, in a temperance speech, said that he was not one of that class who patted the inebriate and thought they could not help drinking. He said that there was no excuse for them, for they could help it. There was only one habit beyond the power of the will,— and that was opium. . . . . .

"I am rejoiced that it is the desire of your heart to be faithful, and to overcome temptations. Without temptation there could be no growth, no aspiration ; it is the successful struggle with these besetments that leads us upward, and enables us to progress in the Divine life. I am pained to say that I quite often fall, instead of overcoming ; indeed, I feel almost weary and discouraged. There is no commandment of my Saviour's that I find it is so hard to obey, as to feel a warm, sympathetic love for those who misjudge me.

From your affectionate mother."

The following letter, it will be noted, is an answer to

one by the redeemed Opium Eater; and by a comparison
of the date of my deliverance, it will be seen that I waited
a sufficient length of time for a recurrence of the desire
or craving for morphine (four or five days) before informing her :—

C*** E********, May 15, 1883.

My Dear Son :—

I cannot express the joy and gratitude with which the
news of your glorious emancipation has filled my heart.   I
am lost in wonder and amazement, bound as you were in
those adamantine chains, and your will so weakened by
this long indulgence, that the chains should be at once
broken, and all appetite and craving taken from you !

Who can ever praise God enough, in time or eternity,
for such a wonderful deliverance !   Peter's chains in prison
were removed in the same way, and all the gates and doors
opened for his freedom.   Some contend that there are no
miracles ; but always, to my mind, when a poor sinner,
sick of sin, lifts his feeble cry to God for help, and gradually becomes transformed with something of the Saviour's
spirit, I feel that a mighty miracle has been performed.
And in your case, it seems in some respects a greater one
than Christ's restoring life to Jairus's daughter, or the
raising of the widow's son to life.

It has made me heartsick as I have read, from time to
time, of the utter hopelessness of expecting reform where
one is sunk under opium's deadly influence.   At such
times I would vehemently implore God to pity your enslaved condition, and break the chains that so relentlessly
bound you.   De Quincy's case was the only one that inspired me with courage, and he was a giant in intellect

and will power. And then to think of God's wonderful goodness in flooding your soul with such peace and happiness, when I supposed that in leaving it off you would for a time suffer all the horrors of delirium!

I long to hear that you are enabled to sleep naturally; and if a reaction takes place from this great peace, do not be discouraged. Christ did not long remain on the mount of transfiguration. It is not our feelings that commend us to Him, but doing His will.

It has seemed as if everything had conspired to keep me from writing to you. Sunday I thought to write, but M. was sent for to go in to Mrs. ——'s, as the night watcher was waiting for some one to take her place, as I got so tired I could not hold my head up, although I did not have much to do. . . . . Poor Mrs. —— died last night, at two o'clock. I think the change of leaving her suffering body must have been pleasant. It has pained me to hear of her gossiping so much, and I have wondered her conscience did not reprove her. It cannot but detract greatly from her spiritual enjoyment. I know that our spirits cannot be changed by merely passing out of our earthly bodies. . . . .

I was really glad to see Willie looking so natural; it did me good. Who knows, if he would follow your example, if he might not be made every whit "whole." Christ is "the life." When He was on earth He healed soul and body at once. . . . .

From your ever affectionate mother.

CHAPTER XX.

MY "GOOD SAMARITAN."

WITH my emancipation from years of bondage and slavery to all the dissipations and vices of worldliness herein enumerated, and feeling in this early hour of triumph malice toward none, and love for the whole human race, and everything of a diverse character having been swallowed up in the immensity of "God is Love," I was ruthlessly awakened by an incident that is worthy of record here as showing the hypocrisy and hate that lurks under a profession of love. My so-called Christian superintendent, who made pretension of Christ's religion, and who said by such acknowledgment that he "loved One whom he has not seen," resorted to all manner of deception and lying to make an excuse for my discharge. And I was not long in affording him the desired opportunity.

Always a firm believer in the principle enunciated by the carpenter's Son, that "the laborer is worthy of his hire," whether he be clothed in the vestments of the priest, or in the just as honorable but the more humble garments of the laborer, there was now every reason why I should be firmer in my belief.

It was now the labor problem in embryo. He had committed himself to the friend who had interested himself in procuring for me the position, by informing him that my work, in quality and quantity, was above criticism ; but in "wage" it was receiving a rate below the scale commonly paid to my fellow-craftsmen. I considered the circumstances under which employment had been given me and the rate of wages paid me munificent, and far in excess of my real merit. Then, too, my organized fellow-workmen had denied me the privilege of their "protection," which practically means the denial of the right to earn one's bread by the sweat of one's brow. Yet until folly's works had wrought havoc in my physical organization, I had for years been a member of the body. And in my fallen state more than once, in distress direful, have I refused the offer of employment where employer and employee were engaged in an unholy struggle for mastership, at the sacrifice of labor's obligation. Yet, ye shades of night! I sought and was debarred reinstatement in the fellowship of my craftsmen! Such is the degrading and debasing influence of alcohol's curse and opium's illusion!

I was, however, satisfied with my hire. My wants were few, and my expenses less. Money was now the drug. Years of profligacy had always drained me of every penny immediately upon receiving it. But every vice gone, and in my humble abode, my salary was more than adequate to supply my needs. A sense of right, however, made it necessary that I should put myself in harmony with the prevailing custom of the established rate of wages paid to men competent to fill the position, and nearly a score of years' labor thereat justified my demand.

It is very easy for one vested with authority to dispose of the services of a fellow-laborer, and my superior had a

simple matter in disposing of the redeemed Opium Eater ;
but it required more lying and hypocrisy than an honest
infidel would ever think of stooping to.

On the 30th day of May, 1883, three weeks after my
emancipation from the opium curse, I found myself discharged from my position, and for no reason that I have
been able to conceive of save the spirit of malice and of
hate.   With an occasional day's work I walked the streets
of Boston for five long and weary months, seeking work
and finding none.   But, of course, full of the new wine of
life, I did not pay that strict diligence in my endeavor that
I might, perhaps, had my circumstances and condition in
life been different.

I might liken my state of mind to that of one suddenly
and unexpectedly liberated from life imprisonment ; of one
receiving sight after years of blindness, or hearing after
deafness, health from sickness, joy from sorrow, or eternal
life after death.

I presume it would be difficult for the black slave to account for the first few months of his liberation from a life
of slavery's curse after the Emancipation Proclamation set
him free.   Everything else was swallowed up in Freedom's
joyful sound !   Yet, after a lapse of eleven years' mingled
grief and sorrow, the happiness and thankfulness experienced by the redeemed Opium Eater in those early days
of his deliverance, is still as fragrant and joyful as are the
youthful periods of reminiscence to those who, having
gone down life's highway and entered the "sere and yellow leaf" on Time's calendar, are happy in recounting the
hours of life's pleasures in the golden days of youth's innocence and happiness.   And while the powers of this

world seemed to have entered into a conspiracy to deprive me of that to which all men should be entitled,—the right to earn one's bread in the God-appointed way, by the sweat of the brow,— yet I found it not.   I found no time, however, for repinings or murmurings, or even to harbor a desire for the fruits of idleness, so great, indeed, was my joy and happiness in my new-found freedom.

The instances where hunger had been appeased, money forthcoming to meet obligations for room rent, etc., when it seemed that my kind and patient creditors must be getting skeptical as to whether I was really in earnest, and making an honest endeavor to obtain employment, were numerous, and other manifestations given of a character that assured me that discipline was one of the kind Heavenly Father's first laws.   But none were so potent in love and encouragement as those I received from the one who had called me to higher and loftier aspirations and holier purposes ; she whose prayers and supplications to her God had never failed, and whose sweet and noble face and words of hope and cheer kept my faltering spirit ever buoyant and happy — Gertrude.

This phase of my life, alone, in those dark and trying days, when I came in contact with skeptical professors of religion, might well be likened to those types made use of by the Saviour, who, in answer to the question, " Who is my neighbor ?" cited the case of a certain man who was passing from Jerusalem to Jericho ; from a close range of observation, religious zealots gazed with eyes of curiosity on the mangled and bleeding form of the victim of thieves and highwaymen without so much as a sympathizing word or look.   But from this true daughter of the Highest, oil and ointment, and balm were poured into my wounds, sweetness and tenderness into my soul, and she never left, nor forsook, nor doubted me ; and although warned by the more worldly, yet outwardly zealous, professors of religion in the church to withdraw her attention and sympathetic support, she never wavered nor faltered in well-doing.

The noblest, and grandest, and purest, and saintliest thing on this beautiful planet of ours,— sin-cursed and full of misery and wretchedness as it is at present,— is a pure and spotless woman, and to this, the highest type of womanhood, this saint belonged.

One who could value and appreciate the exalted character of pure womanhood by contrast was Solomon, and the sublime truths uttered or formulated into proverbs by him are but faint expressions of her true character. Gather them together from every source, fair daughters of earth, and emulate the precepts contained in them ; weave them as garlands about thy brows, and as necklaces may they adorn thy fair throats, that they may bring forth in life the fullness and sweetness of character designed by Him who hath called thee and anointed thee to be the principal factor in destroying the works of darkness !

A kind word, a kind deed, a kind look from a pure and good woman, calls forth respect and honor even though an evil spirit dwells in the hidden flesh of him to whom she speaks ; perchance the mortal may be one whose misdeeds and ill-spent life have brought to him the spirit of sincere repentance. To that other class of foul, demoniacal spirits, bent on seduction and libertinism, even these inhabitants of flesh, and candidates for Hades, are baffled into silence and foiled by this impregnable fortress of Truth — a pure womanhood !

CHAPTER XXI.

THE PRODIGAL'S RETURN.

THE matter contained in this chapter is largely drawn from the writings of the author written during the first year of his emancipation, when with the zeal and fervor of a "new birth" I compiled hundreds of pages incidental of experiences in my life, and the intervening period of time has more forcibly demonstrated the truth then told. As I have often stated, these pages were prompted by a desire and sincere hope of reaching a large class of youthful minds, and pointing with no uncertainty the pathway that lies strewn with human wrecks, burdened with woe and remorse, and whose repentant efforts only too often mock the victim with the returning echoes of their own despairing wail.

I find them dated August 18, 1883, and in a chapter with the caption, "My Conversion," I am forced to pay attention to the manifestations of a nocturnal character in accounting for some of the results therein recorded. The narrative as there found, follows :—

"I deeply and emphatically denied a belief in the hell of the traditionary past — fire and brimstone — as a place of future punishment and torment. Like the great mass of humanity today, I was looking for the Kingdom of God to come by observation. I saw nothing — it was all a great mystery. The past few months of partial reforma-

tion had made little or no impression in solving the doubts
of the ever-recurring question in the soul, 'If a man die,
shall he live again?' In this bewildered state of mind I
one night passed through an experience in dream or vision
that had an awakening influence, and caused me great distress and anxiety of soul. One or two things, however,
before I relate it. Under the influence of morphine there
is a state of bliss and one of corresponding misery. When
the system is charged full of the drug, the sleep is peaceful and sweet, with many beautiful dreams; but as soon
as the drug gets low in the system, so to speak, or the
hours draw near to morning, the mind is often tortured
and disturbed by ugly and frightful dreams. Old and experienced habitués in opium's use do not allow themselves
to get into this side of the scale if they can help it, and this
is one of the main facts of the rapid strides the users of
opiates make in the consumption of them. They invariably see to it that the quantity is not decreased for this reason — it means sleeplessness or bad dreams.

" At this time, especially, was it an easy matter for me to
so handle the drug as largely to avoid the unpleasantness
arising therefrom in ugly dreams; for it was my custom to
arise as early as seven o'clock, and not lie as aforetime long
into the forenoon, or until the effect of the drug was far
spent. It was for this reason and the vividness of the vision
that made me concerned, and at that time tremble at its
significance. Dreams partake largely of natural surroundings. When quite a little boy, a wealthy farmer and
money lender, without sons, and desiring one (and having
a mortgage on my good grandsire's roof, which may, perhaps, have lead him to think he had a pecuniary interest in

his flesh, also), adopted or rather took me, but shortly discovering that I did not have the spirit which he desired in a son, he soon returned me to the maternal roof. He lived on a wild, yet beautiful spot, the house setting on a high elevation of ground, overlooking the grand old Atlantic on Maine's rockbound coast, while not a great distance from the house grew some old and scraggy oaks, quite thickly studded. I seemed to be again at this transient home of unhappiness of my early boyhood, and as I stood gazing upon the scene, it was one that language fails of description. No humanity marred the scene. There in the distance heaved the mighty ocean in all its grandeur, and lashed in fury its rocky barriers, but now intensified by its spiritual brightness. Then I was encompassed about by a garden, the landscape of which was most beautiful to behold. Its flowers, its foliage, its fruits, its beauty, made a paradise of unutterable gorgeousness. I stood transfixed and happy. It was too real to be a dream. I lived an age of bliss in those fleeting moments. Then I was carried along toward the borders of the garden, when, suddenly, I seemed to be enveloped by an atmosphere most chilly and oppressive. It chilled me to the marrow. I looked about me, when I regained my sight, in the now Egyptian darkness that surrounded me, to ascertain the cause of this sudden transition, and found myself in a noisome swamp, horrible, dark and drear. The sudden departure of the luminous brightness had intensified the darkness. As soon as I could discern my position, I found myself among the knarled, and scraggy, and leafless oaks, gigantic in their ugliness. and then the air so foul and damp, it penetrated my very bones. But this was nothing. I looked beneath

my feet.   The sight I saw called forth an agonizing shriek.
There in a mire so soft, in its inky blackness,— all earth
had fled,— so horrible, were countless human beings, and
of a class I could easily recognize.   I had thought that
within my day I had seen in police courts and in the up-
heaval from the haunts of vice, depraved and horrible
specimens of fallen womanhood, but they were nothing in
comparison to those I witnessed here.   They were everywhere.   They seemed to form an endless chain.   As they
each rose to the surface they grasped the great strong
roots of these gigantic monarchs of the forests, and almost
instantly the weight of those beneath broke their hold,
and with one imploring look, sank beneath the slimy surface.   The scene beggars description.   It was horrible.
Then, too, standing as I was on one of those great roots,
with my back pressed hard against its trunk, the clutches
being made to drag me in, was anguish beyond measure.
At last I was seized by my ankles, and with exultant yells
I was being carried down through this slimy, chilly mass,
when my brother, who was awakened by my piteous cries,
with difficulty awoke me.

   "'O thank you, thank you, Willie,' I joyfully cried, as I
realized that I was in the land of the living.   In answer
to his question, I told him he had rescued me from hell.
He quietly rolled over and went to sleep.   Not so with
me.   I was sorely troubled.   I reasoned every way to account for it.   I waited anxiously for some time for the
sound of a clock to tell me the hour.   When I heard the
first peal, I counted breathlessly and anxiously, hoping at
least that it was five ; but when it continued on up to the
midnight hour, I was appalled.   I could not take the com-

"THE SIGHT I SAW CALLED FORTH AN AGONIZING SHRIEK."—(*page 142.*)

forting thought to myself that it arose from a lack of morphine. I had no desire for any, yet I reached forth my hand and took my "hypo" and injected its contents into my arm; but it was no use, I could not sleep, and the burden of my mind was on the after-part of the strange dream. " And this is the place you are willing to go to because you there will have lots of company — the great majority." This was a favorite expression of mine, that if there was a hell, "the majority of mankind would be there." Well, this sight converted me to the minority doctrine; for if all the world had been there that night my anguish could not in any sense have been less complete by their presence.

"Do you believe in such a hell?" I hear the question asked. And I answer emphatically, No!

Its interpretation is simple. The scene of my early boyhood life was indicative of innocence, happiness, and virtue, and the whole journey of life followed out by such a course could bring but an open vision of the goodness of God and the beauty of life, made complete and perfect in the obliterated sting of death and future happiness.

The other picture typified vice, depravity, and utter abandonment — the quintessence of selfishness. The mighty oak, the symbol of power, afforded no protection, for reason was here dethroned; and in the mad rush for place, all were swallowed up by the seething and writhing mass beneath; it was anarchy, rebellion, lawlessness, selfishness, greed, hopelessness, and was also typical of the world as it is today, in its social and political corruptness, which in its blindness and unreasoning greed is rushing into the same chaotic bosom of unrighteousness which they have builded for it in this life.

*　　*　　*　　*　　*　　*

I further quote from this manuscript of "My Conversion" the subjoined: "Being out of employment, I embraced the opportunity of visiting my home, or rather that of grandfather's, where my mother resided. I was once more returning to that spot where I had passed much of my boyhood; again, where scarcely two years previous, a confirmed opium eater, wrecked and penniless and wellnigh friendless, save my mother, and she unable to render assistance, I had been driven forth by relentless poverty at the mandate of the good old man. It was just. It was as he had said, 'Impossible to have me longer about the place; it encouraged idleness, and he was receiving no recompense.' I dressed well. But then, purple and fine linen in the shape of broadcloth and tailor-made suits, are often but an ill-concealed covering for the shams and rottenness that lurk beneath them, and fit companions for the glib and lying tongues of their masqueraders. He knew not the load under which I staggered. An explanation would not have brought to him a conception of its truth. He had heard of my riches, now he knew I did not meet my obligations. He could not account for it. Had he lived ninety odd years, and such things had never happened to him! Then, too, infancy had wellnigh returned, and he had nearly completed the cycle of years, and was about to enter into that unknown sphere from out which he came nearly a century before. [He died in his ninety-eighth or ninety-ninth year.]

"It was, indeed, the Prodigal's return. He gladly welcomed me. I stopped but a few days. My poverty would not allow of a longer stay. Of course, religion and conversions had their part. Familiar with his thoughts and doctrines, and having crossed them as a boy, as the reader will recall, I studiously avoided coming in conflict with them now. 'Just as the twig is bent the tree's inclined,' and with ninety years passed in the shade of Calvinism and Puritan righteousness he looked with keen suspicion on any 'new-fangled' ideas not in harmony with those hoary traditions. I would not here narrate for the reader a minute detail of his conviction and conversion if I could, for to do justice to the theme would require exact transcription. Suffice it to say, it was one of the 'old-fashioned' kind of more than a century ago. His life from infancy had been surrounded by a halo of Puritan righteousness — ministers and devout men and women for associates; he was born religious. At the age of twelve he was a member of the church of which for seventy years, more or less, he was deacon — a distinction which he was very proud of. No profanity had ever escaped his lips under the greatest provocation; to him it would have been blasphemy, and well-nigh unpardonable. A chaste life, none of the sins imputed to the characters he loved so dearly to read of in God's Word, and which he condoned, had ever been his. And yet this upright and good and moral young man had such a conversion at nineteen, as to make one shudder. He was compelled to give up his business, and for days suffered the tortures of the damned, and for his sins! At last he found peace, and his testimony and experience were the bright particular spots in his life ever after.

"Is it at all to be wondered at that his own children and children's children were not solicitous for salvation at such a price? Then, too, if this life, immaculate in its existence, so to speak, was compelled to purchase peace at so frightful a cost, where was the ungodly sinner with the moral courage to think or even desire it at an intensified ratio!

"After listening to the familiar recital of his conversion, which he had been repeating for seventy years, my sinful existence must have presented itself to his mind, for he said, with evident misgivings, 'A man who has lived the terribly sinful and unholy life you have confessed to, must have had great contrition and remorse of conscience for your sins?'

"'My sins! my sins! Why, I have never thought anything about them!' I replied, innocently.

"'Never thought anything about them! Never thought anything about them!' he exclaimed in blank amazement.

"'No, sir,' I thoughtfully answered.

"He was astonished. I must confess that I was, too. If what I had all my life long been accustomed to hear was a result of 'conversion,' surely I had cause for anxiety. If, too, my sins were to trouble me in like manner as they were supposed to every genuinely converted man, my remaining days would be passed in a state of mind little short of lunacy and would be a curse instead of a blessing. My past sins did not trouble me, and I did not propose to trouble my sins. I felt more than satisfied to leave them in the past if they had no objection to thus being isolated.

[The Good Book for ninety odd years had reiterated to this devout man that "SIN WAS THE TRANSGRESSION OF LAW." His life had been prolonged to that of nearly a centenarian by conformity to the law of right living. By the transgression of the vital principles of the same righteous and eternal law, they had ground me to powder, so to speak, at the age of thirty-three years. I have sinned; I have suffered. These pages but feebly express how much. His environment and early religious inclination had been largely the factors in his preservation; whereas the opposite conditions had brought to me my physical as well as moral dethronement.]

"At the end of my short visit I returned to Boston. Immediately following mutual greetings, my brother startled me with the information that his attention had been called to a newspaper paragraph setting forth the illegality of my marriage and suits for the recovery of the property. But he could tell me nothing definite about the matter.

"I could see in the imaginings of my then supersensitive mind many things confirmatory of the truthfulness of my brother's story. Then, too, of all things in my life, I desired the burial of this sad history forever. I would have made any sacrifice, had I been able, to bury the whole business. It worried me. I stood the pressure of my feelings till late in the afternoon, when I resolved upon my course of action. I was a candidate for church membership. I would not join any church until this matter was out of the way. There was nothing dishonorable about it from a worldly standpoint. I felt different, however, toward the Church. It was Christ's body, and I would bring no part of my unholy life into it nor disgrace the name of Christian, until this affair was satisfactorily settled.

"Thus determined, I set off immediately to see the pastor of the church to which my name had been presented, with the resolution of unfolding the true state of things, and getting his advice. The clergyman was not at home. His wife, however, met me cordially, and, no doubt, perceiving that I was in sore distress, and being a woman of much tact and experience, I was soon confiding my trouble to her. She listened with close attention, asking few questions, until I had finished. I think it must have been one of the greatest revelations she ever listened to, for she gave expression to her mental cogitations in words like these: 'We little know what our children are coming to. Poverty is preferable, perhaps, for them than wealth and luxury, with its temptations and degradations.'

"She acquiesced in my thought that it would be better to wait until the matter was finally settled before uniting with the church, and also decided to rehearse the matter over with her husband. I returned to my room. I have vague recollections that my open confession brought no peace to my soul. I felt miserable indeed. My sins had found me out, and had come to trouble me. My grandfather might be right, after all. I was not going to lose sleep over it, and that night an experience came to me that settled the sin question with me for the past, present and the future; and nearly a dozen years of life since that memorable night have demonstrated to me the infallible truth of the vision. I find it difficult to transcribe the picture into type, although the grandeur, and beauty, and clearness of the scene is indelibly impressed on my mind.

"I seemed to be in a large room, yet it had neither ceiling nor walls. Gradually there poured into it a light, the soft and mellow brightness of which far outshone the light of things terrestrial, and must have been celestial. I was in a reclining position. I was conscious of the presence of a being, and heard and recognized a voice. The

"IN RAISED LETTERS OF GOLD, THE WORD 'FORGIVEN!'"—(*page 149.*)

vision was subdivided into three parts, representative of sins — past, present and future. Looking off into space, there passed before me scrolls of exquisite workmanship, each graduating smaller than its predecessor, and on each, in raised letters of gold, the word 'Forgiven!' The personage, who stood at my head on the right, and who was shielded from my view, told me the meaning of the scrolls, which were typical of my recorded sins, which had all been canceled or forgiven. This signified my past life, and ended the first part. Of course, it is needless to remark that I was very happy. The scene shifted, and I was again in the gay and frivolous world, drinking from the fountains of unhallowed pleasures. I had fallen, and the darkness that encircled me and the remorse and anguish that filled my soul was terrible in the extreme. After remaining in this state of wretchedness for what seemed an endless period of time, I again found myself enveloped in this halo of light, and my visitant informed me that, having a knowledge of right, and doing wrong, henceforth this would be my condition. In other words, if I again yielded to my passions, I would suffer this remorse of conscience, or the unhappy state. This ended the second part, or present transgression. 'But,' said my instructor, 'Satan has kept a record of your life,' and thereupon there passed before me other scrolls, none the less beautiful in design, yet black as night in their composition, all lettered in gold, and bearing legends thereon in harmony with acts of my fast life, such as 'Opium Eater,' 'Drunkard,' 'Profligate,' 'Gambler,' etc., down to the very minutest sins; 'and,' continued my teacher, 'he will flay you with them until the end of your days; but if you con-

tinue faithful in the Lord Jesus Christ, you shall be saved.'
I awoke.   The burden was gone.   I was extremely happy.

"It was all very simple, and the dignity and manner of
the messenger was what one might expect where law and
order reigned.   It was a simple kindergarten lesson of life.
'Where there is no vision, the people perish ; but he that
keepeth the law, happy is he,' saith the proverb.

"The next morning, I ascertained from my counsel that
my fears were groundless, and that a case bearing some of
its characteristics, and having a name similar to my own,
had misled my brother, he only having a superficial knowledge of the matter.   Then, too, the probationary period
suggested by my kind friend, in regard to my deferring
the time of uniting with the church until my transgressions were unlikely to annoy, has left an indefinite period
of time in the future for me to comply in this regard."

*   *   *   *   *   *

Three years after the incidents recorded in the foregoing, I again visit the scenes of my youth and my beloved
mother and aged kinsman.   I no longer walked alone, and
the companion of my journey was none other than the
noble woman who had rescued and sustained me in my
faltering and flagging moments—Gertrude.   On her bosom
there nestled a tiny soul ; divinely beautiful and pure
they were to me.   What a contrast had been my life in
comparison with these !   How often have I been flayed
by my knowledge in this particular sense !   How often
have I been impressed with the righteousness of the plea
for one standard of morality for man as well as for woman !
My past life to her was as though it had never been.
And in the sunshine and happiness of her life, it was at

times like an almost forgotten and ill-remembered dream.
And while every trace of that past sinful life had been
obliterated by an Omnipotent power, yet the golden gift
of remembrance has never ceased to hold before my eyes
the hideous pictures of the past !

But the child. One day the aged great-grandsire had
folded the little lump of fragrance, and beauty, and purity
in his arms. I sat near them, and after talking in a very
unique, childish way to the little stranger, who appeared
to be trying to fathom his patriarchal bearing, he raised
the child in his arms, and solemnly said, "God bless the
little child, and watch over her, and preserve her, and
may she be a child of the Lord !" The divine spark is
small in the human soul where there is no love for little
children.

There was a striking contrast in the picture before me.
The old Puritan had walked almost a hundred years in the
world, yet he was not far removed in actual knowledge of
what was in it from that of the infant in his arms ! Yet,
on the other hand, there is no similarity between old age
and infancy. No more and just as much as there is between the budding foliage of spring and the sere and yellow leaf of autumn. His whole life had been shapen in
strong convictions, and in the near hour of his departure
they were as tenaciously adhered to as the smouldering
embers of life gave him warmth to express them. The
thoughts regarding faith and doctrine that he had been
taught in youth were the alpha and omega of Truth, and
in my zeal on my first visit I had made an attempt to controvert some of his youthful teachings by the Scriptures,
and I shall not soon forget the look of stern severity and

commiseration as he informed me ".that he had read the
Bible through almost as many times as I had lived years ;
and did I presume to teach him ?"   It was another way
of giving expression to the thought, " Thou wast altogether born in sin, and dost thou teach us ?"

Then this second childhood—if such it can be called—
narrated incidents of his youth, his early manhood, and how
in the birth and loss of little ones they had been made the
immediate factors of his instituting divine worship in the
family circle and instructing them in religious duty, that
showed little by contrast with the bunch of sweetness and
innocence that lay cooing and toying in her mother's arms
beside this type of second childhood.

"Most of my children died in infancy or early childhood
(I thought I detected a gleam of satisfying light pass over
his wrinkled countenance), before Satan had power to lure
and snare them, and drag their souls down to perdition.
All the others have 'rejected the overtures of mercy' and
denied 'the Lord that bought them with a price' except
your mother (a shade of uncertainty seemed to disturb him
even in her case), and unless 'they sue for pardon,' they
will be poor, wretched, miserable lost sinners." And Dives
in torment was to be their state through countless ages !

I quietly made an attempt to rescue one of the departed
ones from the lurid flames of such a monstrous fate.   She
was my mother's younger sister.   Intellectually endowed,
her accomplishments were many ; but none were more
marked than the true dignity of her womanhood and her
motherhood, and together with a personality of rare beauty,
her character was so sweet and noble that the fragrance
of heaven could but be augmented by her presence.

"But Aunt Ellen, surely, was a faithful, conscientious child of God," I had the courage to intimate.

"She was a kind, affectionate daughter, a most lovable and beautiful woman. But she denied her Lord and Master and 'put him to an open shame,'" he said, in a tone of pathetic sadness.

"How was that?" I asked, for I did not remember having heard much, if anything, about her religious creed. I was soon enlightened, however.

He said that she had become identified with Unitarianism.

To this noble old Puritan, this "ism," together with Universalism, and, in fact all the numerous "isms," except his own true "ism," was heresy run mad! There was no consolation left to this aged disciple of Calvin after so radical a departure from his own faith to one of so heterodoxical a tendency.

I had not then, neither have I now, any desire to modify the condition of the parable made use of by God's dear Son in typifying the state of blessedness on the one hand, and the self-invited punishment of an arrogant and selfish Dives on the other, but rather to give that meed of justice to this sweet and patient life for one in well-doing; but the seed fell on stony ground.

*   *   *   *   *   *

On another occasion my grandfather was bemoaning the lost condition of his two sons. They surely had departed from the faith of their worthy sire. But in the world of business and in social life they were honored. In season and out of season, however, this zealous disciple importuned and warned them "to flee from the wrath to come."

Where there is an absolute uncertainty with reference to the fixedness of a matter, it is far better to inspire one with hope than to surrender all to despair. It would, of course, have been sheer madness on my part to attempt to bring consolation to the old man's heart by quoting the hope abundantly to be found to meet this very need out of the Scriptures, for his vast number of readings of them precluded such a venture. I thought I was so well fortified with a theme, and that the potency of my argument would be sufficient to win the battle without resorting to them more than casually.

"Ye shall know them by their fruits," said Christ.

Both of them, however, were content to walk the even tenor of their way and remain true to their convictions outside the professing pale of the Church, rather than enter her not believing in her dogmas, as they had been instructed to believe in their youth.

My plea was made largely, too, for a suspension of judgment, for it is better to err on mercy's side in our reasonings than to do injustice to a fellow-mortal.

For more than thirty years one of the sons had not looked upon his aged father's face. He resided in one of the largest and worldliest cities of the Union, and was a part of its life. He had a family, and by no means an economical one. His income was a salaried one. I drew the picture of city life to the old man, with its theaters, balls and gay parties, the palatial drinking palace, the gilded gambling hell, the pandemonium of stock gambling, political intrigues and malfeasance in office, "confidence" men and women, Bacchanalian temples of lust which would put to shame those of ancient Israel, Mammon worshipped

in the temples reared to God, and where in the mad rush
of life, father and mother, brother and sister, were often
lost sight of and forgotten in the intense earnestness for
wealth on the one hand, and to outshine in gorgeous splen-
dor and luxurious extravagance the world around them on
the other.

The old Puritan groaned at Satan's power !

" But in all these surroundings, your son has been loyal
to God's ' first commandment with promise '—' Honor thy
father and thy mother'—and for thirty years, with clocklike
precision, through adversity as well as prosperity, his purse
has always been opened.   Through his generosity and un- .
selfish manhood, the fire on the hearth sends forth its warm
and genial glow, the larder replenished with the good things
of life, the greed of the usurer satisfied, and your roof left
to shelter you in your departing hours ; the tax-gatherer,
too, is satisfied from the same self-sacrificing hand.   When
to a better world your loved companion was taken, your
stream of life flowed on unbroken, aided by hands not
less loving and dutiful.   Gladly, too, has this lost son con-
tributed of his means that your longings in the spiritual
way might find consolation, while the recipients of his
bounty reserved for him the endless companionship of the
Dives of past and coming time !

" Even David rejoiced, under the burden of his great
transgression, that his soul was not always to be left in hell,
and that with others he would be ' comforted ' in the pit.
And who will say that the matchless love of that royal
descendant of David — Jesus Christ, unto whom all power
was given — would rest content until the full fruition of
that hope had found realization ?

"If, then, God hath made such promises,— and it looks fair and reasonable to suppose that He did,— whom hath He ever authorized to make null and void so just, so loving, and so merciful a decree, and where may it be found?"

The old man's features softened by turns, and I felt I had touched a vulnerable point in his traditionary armor; but, alas! the weak points were re-enforced, and my honest endeavor found no lodgment in his breast nor thanks from his lips.

But from the maternal fount of life there had gone forth the leaven that was to harmonize the whole lump!

* * * * * *

The old Puritan died, and went to his grave in full age, like as a shock of corn cometh in in his season. He stood, like his progenitors, for all things that make for righteousness; for a clean manhood and a pure womanhood, and for an upright business integrity that never was dishonored. He was impoverished and kept poor by giving credit to the unfortunate, and to others whom a sagacious business man would not have trusted for the price of a red herring. There was no cant nor hypocrisy in his faith; he believed it with a tenacity worthy of a far better hope. He was a fearless man. Yet that fearlessness was not begotten of "perfect Love." Warm and sympathetic affection was not in his nature. He was an Old Testament saint rather than a New. He would put to flight the armies of the aliens by the strategy of war, rather than by faith and gospel reasoning. He was a total abstainer, and lived to see the greatest breach of etiquette (not to place before the pastor of the flock the decanter of the choicest liquor) made equally a breach of decorum to have done so.

He was an Abolitionist. The only one to give him battle was a "copperhead"–infidel and near neighbor; driven from pillar to post by the old Puritan's unanswerable constitutional arraignment of the relic of barbarism, the copperhead would make a futile attempt to bolster up his "lost cause" out of the Book, and finally rounded off with the common vulgarisms of the times, in regard to eating, and sleeping and marrying. Yet no profanity would ever escape his lips in the old man's presence, but beyond his hearing he gave vent to his pent-up feelings in this particular. This old Puritan, the last of his race, stood for a Sabbath that had in it a day of rest for man and beast; an open Bible, the public schools, the freedom of all men; and last, but not least, the Diadem of Liberty, the heritage bequeathed by a noble ancestry to all mankind who honor and revere this inestimable birthright vouchsafed to them for all time. And blind indeed is he, and cannot see afar off, who would put forth his hand to snatch the least one of these jewels from the Crown of Human Liberty; for the Spirit of the Puritan and the Pilgrim is not dead, but in a broader and more comprehensive form it will work out the destiny of Him who called it forth out of obscurity, and has made it the symbol of hope and the desire of all nations!

CHAPTER XXII.

"MULTUM IN PARVO."

" Today, 'tis happy sunshine;
   Tomorrow, clouds and rain;
The heart now beats with pleasure,
   Anon it throes with pain.

Awhile we have our dear ones,
   And then we have them not;
Only a memory keeps them—
   They cannot be forgot.

This golden gift, remembrance,
   When once the grave is crossed,
Will be our guiding angel
   To find what we have lost!"

THE "Opium Eater" can here take leave of his reader, so far as the abandonment of, and successful accomplishment and restoration to complete physical health from, the morphine habit, alcoholism, and use of tobacco are concerned, and the triumphant overcoming of those vices and passions that follow so rapidly and swiftly in the wake of their indulgence, by that revelation that came to him through the manifestations of the Spirit and power of God in the manner described. No return to any one of them has ever taken place. So far as morphia is concerned, no reminiscences of the past bring longings or even a thought or a desire to again enter the inferno through which he has passed. The others are with me.

They are a part of my being ; they belong to the house in which I live, to be conquered and subdued. Without them there would be no growth, and to subject the passions to the laws of right living is, indeed, the chief end of life. The years that have intervened are years that have been crowded with the real issues of life,—the struggle for subsistence, for the care of wife and children, and the making of a home — the grandest institution ever devised among men by our loving Heavenly Father. Yea, more than this, in the beneficent goodness of God, who gave me for a companion this true and noble woman, my rescuer — Gertrude — my life was divinely blessed. He honored that union by one of His greatest gifts to mankind—offspring. And He that gave, exercised the divine right of taking to Himself that which He had created. Beautiful and lovely indeed were the angel forms that fascinated the redeemed Opium Eater's life with a far greater enchantment than any of the forms of pleasure and of unhallowed passion in his prodigal life. One by one they came and lent their sunshine, their sweetness and their fragrance to buoy up and gladden my heart and make joyous my soul. One by one, He in whose hands all life is, and who meets out mercy and judgment with loving kindness, took them to Himself.

And tonight, as I close this part of my life,— an epitome of eleven years of redeemed life,— all that is left to me of my family is the sleeping innocent and motherless child before me ; greater in her unconscious power of love than all the powers of passion that swayed me for evil and abandonment ! Such is man's love for his offspring ! Who, then, can fathom God's love for poor erring humanity ?

In the silent city of the dead, "dust to dust," the mortal forms of wife and children, mother, and brothers lie,—unknown, unmarked, and unremembered by the devices that keep vigil for a brief period the name of the silent mortal mouldering back to earth beneath them. Yet they live, and are far greater factors in my life, perhaps, than they would be if clothed in tabernacles of clay and present with me.

The following lines I found within the lids of my wife's Bible long after her death,—a book, by the way, which from the numberless passages marked by this young saint, had been kept for use instead of ornament,—and as the sentiments expressed in them are typical of her life and devotion to my eternal welfare and her simple faith, I deem them a fitting close to this painful and feebly told narrative :—

> "I 'll think of thee when the day of grief is thine ;
> Should the fierce blast e'er overwhelm thy heart,
> The words of comfort spoken shall be mine,
> And gladly of thy care I 'll bear a part.
>
> I 'll think of thee whene'er thou art alone,
> And all thy youthful days and friends are fled ;
> The voice to cheer thy solitude, my own,
> In sickness watch with love around thy bed.
>
> I'll think of thee when life is yielding to decay—
> In my last prayer I will remember thee.
> Wilt thou, then, when I am resting with the dead
> Forget her not who loved to think of thee?
>
> And if God takes thee first to be with Him
> To swell the company of saints forgiven,
> And leaves me for a space to war with Sin,
> I 'll think of thee, and come to thee in Heaven."

APPENDIX.

I trust that enough has been revealed in the preceding pages to forever deter every reader from any desire to make a practical experiment with opium in any form to demonstrate the truth or falsity of this record. Remember, that years of indulgence destroyed hope, peace, and happiness, and brought wretchedness and suffering indescribable to the Opium Eater, and only a quickened life by God's power has sent this description back to mortal eyes. It is only the confirmed opium slave who, hardened by years of excesses, in the following pages portrays his master, not the novice. He cannot acquire this knowledge by a single indulgence, any more than a mechanic acquires a trade by a few days' occupation thereat, or an actor become an artist by an occasional appearance before the footlights. Years of toil in the one case, patient perseverance in the other, must be given ; and, likewise, experience alone makes known the dark despair, the horror, and the agony of the opium eater's true state. As the inspired revelator uncovers the torments of the damned in the nether world in the Apocalypse, so it has been my endeavor to make bare a like existence in this through the opium habit, and to the same end—salvation by prevention.

While I produce here but a few cases from the recorded volumes of evidence, I might supply their places by living examples with which I have been made conversant during the past ten years,— tales I would fain burn from my memory, and consequently avail myself of those that are none the less real, simply from the fact that they live only in cold type.

When one of the preacher–poet's most steadfast friends and admirers (Mr. Cottle) learned that he was addicted to this curse of opium using, he dwelt long upon the subject with indescribable sorrow, and finally determined to brave everything and make an effort to save him. He addresses a long letter to him, full of interest and sympathy, and that which follows are extracts taken from Coleridge's reply, and draws its own pathetic picture :—

LETTERS OF COLERIDGE.

"———, April 26, 1814.

" DEAR SIR,—

" You have poured oil into the raw and festering wound of an old friend's conscience, Cottle,—but it is the *oil of vitriol!* I but barely glanced at the middle of the first page of your letter, and have seen no more of it ; not from resentment,— God forbid !— but from the state of my bodily and mental suffering, that scarcely permitted human fortitude to let in a new visitor of affliction.

" The object of my present reply is to state the case just as it is,— first, that for ten years the anguish of my spirit has been indescribable, the sense of my danger staring, but the consciousness of my guilt worse — far worse than all ! I have prayed, with drops of agony on my brow ; trembling not only before the justice of my Maker, but even before the mercy of my Redeemer. ' I gave thee so many talents, what hast thou done with them ?' . . .

" Suffice it to say that effects were produced which acted on me by terror and cowardice of pain and sudden death, not (so help me God !) by any temptation of pleasure, or

expectation or desire of exciting pleasurable sensations.
. . . Such intolerable restlessness and incipient bewil-
derment, that in the last of my attempts to abandon the
dire poison I exclaimed in agony, which I now repeat in
seriousness and solemnity, 'I am too poor to hazard this!"
. . . Now there is no hope! O God, how willingly
would I place myself under Dr. Fox in his establishment!
for my case is a species of madness, only that it is a de-
rangement, an utter impotence of the volition, and not of
the intellectual faculties. You bid me rouse myself. Go,
bid the man paralytic in both arms, to rub them briskly
together, and that will cure him. 'Alas!' he would reply,
'that I cannot move my arms is my complaint and my
misery!' S. T. COLERIDGE."

—:o:—

The subjoined letter from Coleridge to Cottle still further sheds light on the terrible folly of becoming a slave
to the essence of that little soporific plant, described by
Shakspeare thus —

> " Within the infant rind of this small flower,
> Poison hath residence, and medicine power."

"BRISTOL, June 22, 1814.

"DEAR SIR,—

I am unworthy to call any good man friend,— much less
you, whose hospitality and love I have abused ; accept,
however, my entreaties for your forgiveness and your
prayers.

"Conceive a poor, miserable wretch who for many years
has been attempting to beat off pain by a constant recurrence to the vice that produces it. Conceive a spirit in
hell employed in tracing out for others the road to that
heaven from which his crimes excluded him. In short,
conceive whatever is most wretched, helpless, and hopeless, and you will form as tolerable a notion of my state
as it is possible for a good man to have.

"I used to think the text in St. James that 'he who offends in one point, offends in all,' very harsh ; but I now feel the awful, the tremendous truth of it.

"In the one crime of Opium, what crimes have I not made myself guilty of ? Ingratitude to my Maker ! and to my benefactor, injustice ! and unnatural cruelty to my poor children !—self-contempt for my repeated promises— breach, nay, too often, actual falsehood.

"After my death, I earnestly entreat that a full and un- qualified narrative of my wretchedness, and of its guilty cause, may be made public, that at least some little good may be effected by the direful example.

"May God Almighty bless you, and have mercy on your still affectionate, and in his heart grateful,

S. T. COLERIDGE."

*_**

I quote a short paragraph from the biography of John Randolph of Virginia :—

JOHN RANDOLPH AND THE OPIUM HABIT.

"Mr. Randolph made no secret of his use of opium at this time (1831). 'I live by, if not upon opium,' said he to a friend. He had been driven to it as an alleviation of pain to which few mortals were doomed. He could not now dispense with its use. 'I am sinking fast,' said he, 'into an opium-eating sot ; but, please God, I will shake off the incubus yet before I die ; for whatever difference of opinion may exist on the subject of suicide, there can be none as to the rushing into the presence of our Creator in a state of drunkenness, whether produced by opium or brandy."

*_**

A BITTER EXPERIENCE.

The extract following relates to the case of a gentle- man, some forty years ago, who had been for eight years addicted to the use of opium, and who had made three ineffectual attempts to abandon it, and was sent back to his nepenthe in a state of almost suicidal despair only after the torture had continued for weeks without a moment's mitigation. It is written by Fitz Hugh Ludlow, a writer of eminence, both in science and letters, and appeared in Harper's Magazine in August, 1867, the article being entitled " What Shall They Do to be Saved ?" He too was an unfortunate opium user, as well as a physician, and, what is quite often the case, practiced on others for that which he could find no balm for himself. The Opium Eater, in his experience in looking for assistance in his dire extremity, has twice been under treatment by men, since deceased, one suicidally, who were addicted to the same habit as himself. " Physician, heal thyself," might aptly have applied in their cases, and in many others today :

" I have just returned from forty-eight hours' friendly and professional attendance at a bedside, where I would place every young person in this country for a single hour before the Responsibilities of Life have become the sentinels, and Habit the Jailer of his Will. . . . For the ninety days he had been going without opium, he had known nothing like proper sleep. I desire to be understood with mathematical literalness. There had been no period when he had been semi-conscious ; when the outline of things in his room grew vaguer, and for five minutes he had a dull sensation of not knowing where he was. This temporary numbness was the only state in all that time that simulated sleep. From the hour he first refused his cravings and went to the battlefield of bed, he had endured such agony as I believe no man but the opium eater has ever known. I am led to believe that the records of fatal lesion, mechanical childbirth, cancerous affection, the stake itself, contain no greater torture than a confirmed opium eater experiences on getting free. Popularly, this suffering is supposed to be purely intellectual,—but nothing can be wider of the truth. Its intellectual part is bad enough, but the physical symptoms are appalling beyond representation. The look on the face of the opium sufferer is, indeed, one of such keen mental anguish, that outsiders may well be excused for supposing that to be all.

"I shall never forget to my dying day that awful Chinese face which actually made me rein my horse at the door of an opium *hong* where it appeared, after a night's debauch, at six o'clock one morning, when I was riding on the outskirts of a Pacific city. It spoke of such a nameless horror in its owner's soul, that I made the sign of a pipe, and proposed, in 'pigeon' English, to furnish the necessary coin. The Chinaman sank down on the steps of the *hong*, like a man hearing medicine proposed to him when he was gangrened from head to foot, and made a gesture, palms downward toward the ground, as one who said, ' It has done its last for me ; I am paying the matured bills of penalty.' The man had exhausted all that opium could give him ; and now, flattery past, the strong one kept his goods in peace. When the most powerful alleviative known to medical science has bestowed the last Judas kiss which is necessary to emasculate its victim, and, sure of its prey, substitutes stabbing for blandishment, what alleviation, stronger than the strongest, should soothe such doom ?

"I may give chloroform. I always do in the *denouement* of bad cases,—ether — nitrous oxyde. In employing the first two agents I secure rest, but I induce death in nine cases out of ten.

"I have said that during the first month of trial my friend had not a moment of even partial unconsciousness. Since that time there has been, perhaps, ten occasions a day when for a period of one minute in length to five his poor, pain-wrinkled forehead sank on his couch, his eyes fell shut, and to outsiders he seemed asleep. But that which appeared sleep was internally, to him, only one stupendous succession of horrors, which confusedly succeeded each other for apparent eternities of being, and ended with some nameless catastrophe of woe or wickedness, in a waking more fearful than the state volcanically ruptured by it. During the nights I sat by him, these occasional relaxations, as I learned, reached their maximum length—my familiar presence acting as a sedative,—but from each of them he woke bathed in perspiration from sole to crown, shivering under alternate flashes of cold and heat, mentally confused to a degree which for half an hour rendered every object in the room unnatural and terrible to him; a nervous jerk which threw him quite out of bed, and with a cry of agony, as loud as any under amputation, although in his waking state two men were requisite to move him.

"In the case of this patient the treatment was abandoned, and the use of opium resumed, but the sufferer died in a short time, unable to recover from the shock caused by discontinuing the use of the drug."

And in closing the narrative of this case, Dr. Ludlow says: "As I dropped my friend's wasted hand and stepped to the threshold, he repeated the request he had often made to me, saying:—

"It is almost like Dives seeking for a messenger to his brethren; but tell them,—tell all *young* men what it is that they come not into this torment."

**

A TYPICAL CASE OF ATTEMPTED SELF-CURE.

The statement which follows is taken from a pamphlet, which has done duty as an advertising medium for an "opium cure." The words are largely borrowed, without credit, from works on this subject, and from various articles published in magazines. Not being anxious to advance the sale of the "nostrum" by advertising its puta-

tive author, I also use it without credit to the writer.
The experiences narrated, however, are duplicates in the
lives of innumerable persons, who somewhere in their descending course make an effort to abandon the drug :—

" The opium user remembers that it was by means of
doses gradually increased that he came to be a confirmed
habitué, and he argues with himself that as he entered the
regions of horror step by step, down a descending path,
so he may retrace the long and steep incline, and, finding
at its top the 'gates of ingress' still open, may pass out
into a free and happy life!

" Easy is it to glide down into the awful opium gulf, but
to return and escape — how hard! The recorded experiences of opium and morphine users who have attempted
to cure themselves by gradual reductions of the daily dose
of their opiate, is like a horrible, infernal chorus of shrieks
and screams. The language has been ransacked by these
sufferers for terms intense enough to set forth even a
little of their misery!

" Let me endeavor to place before the reader the experiences of a typical case of attempted self-cure. Every
incident and detail of suffering, and of lamentable and
disastrous failure, can be substantiated by scores of published experiences. Let the individual be of middle age,
and originally of more than ordinary strength of constitution, and of a hopeful temperament. His powers have not
been greatly wasted, as yet, and he has by nature a strong
mind and a determined will. He has hitherto made only
feeble and abortive attempts to cease using the drug, but
now, alarmed by a failing stomach, or shocked by a vision
of a life ruined, he summons all his strength and con-
denses all his energies of mind and body into a resolution
to break all the withes which are binding all his powers.
He withdraws himself from his accustomed duties and
cares, so that he may be burdened by no unnecessary

weight in the contest, and begins to carry out his determination to reduce, gradually, his daily "ration" of the
poison until the amount taken shall become so insignificant that he can entirely abandon it.   He makes rapid reductions the first few days .   .   .   but he does not know
that the perverted machinery of his body has been storing
up morphine in all the tissues, and that it is this hoarded
poison which makes the first stages of his trial so easy by
supplying the stimulus which the system has come to require.   This store of isomerized morphine soon begins to
fail, and although it might require weeks to entirely ex-
haust it, the help which it gives becomes less and less.
From this time, be his daily reductions ever so minute, the
sufferer rapidly passes into the seething crater of the
opium agony.   He experiences an intense irritability, both
mental and physical ; cold chills pierce to his very marrow,
to be suddenly succeeded by hot flashes and outbursts of
perspiration, which make him drip at every pore.   Pains
which pierce and sting like poisoned spears are felt here
and there all over the body.   In the stomach there is a
constant, terrible sensation, as if a pack of sharp-toothed,
hungry wolves were gnawing and tearing its coat.   The
mind becomes affected.   The power of attention and continuous thought is lost ; reading becomes impossible, not
merely on account of ceaseless restlessness and tormenting pains, but because the mental faculties are incapable
of concentration, and it is impossible to fix the attention
upon consecutive sentences.   All mental activity is paralyzed.   Consciousness remains, but it is a consciousness
of unceasing pain.   There is no longer any restful sleep,
but only half slumber, and this is full of conscious uneasiness, or is tormented with delirious dreams.

And yet, this is but the threshold of the torture chamber.   As the days pass, and with stubborn endurance, the
reductions are still made, the patient experiences horrors
which no words can portray ! For a brief period after
taking his comparatively minute doses of the drug, he may

experience some mitigation of his sufferings, but the relief is only partial and exceedingly brief.   Not for an instant does his torment cease, and day and night not a conscious moment is he free from pains, like those which, in darker ages than this, wrenched shrieks and awful secrets from victims tortured on the rack.   If the eyelids close, it is not in slumber,— the drug which once gave such sweet and irresistible invitation to repose, has performed its treachery — it has "murdered sleep."

The description closes thus : "It may aid the reader to form some adequate notion of the dreary length to which these nights draw themselves along, to mention that on one occasion I resolved neither to look at the clock nor open my eyes for the next two hours.   It lacked ten minutes to one.   .   .   .   For what seemed thousands upon thousands of times, I listened to the clock's steady ticking.   I heard it repeat, with murderous iteration, ' Ret-ri-bu-tion,' varied occasionally, under some new access of pain, with other utterances.   .   .   .   With these allotted tasks accomplished, and with the suspicion that the allotted hours must have long expired, I would yet remind myself that I was in a condition to exaggerate the lapse of time ; and then, to give myself every assurance of fidelity to my purpose, I would start off on a new term of endurance.   I seemed to myself to have borne the penance for hours, to have made myself a shining example of what a resolute will can do under circumstances the most inauspicious. At length, when certain that the time must have more than expired, and with no little elation over the happy result of the experiment, I looked up at the clock and found it to have been just three minutes past one !"

And every second of those interminable minutes is full of indescribable pain.   The feet and lower limbs seem filled—not with blood, but with fire.   The nerves, so long held in unnatural quiet, awake and begin at once to pay, with interest, for every moment of enforced, abnormal torpor, with intensest torture in every atom of their fibre.

A fierce, insatiable restlessness pervades every particle of the body—constant motion through each day and night is a necessity, but in no wise a relief.

***

The following brief extracts, in regard to the use of opium for a long term of years, by William Wilberforce, that wonderful character who achieved the most eminent renown and imperishable honor in his ceaseless warfare on the traffic of human flesh in the British Empire, and who lived to see his efforts crowned with success, was an opium slave; the case of a man's use of the drug for a half a century; and also the experience of one who writes from the standpoint of having vanquished his foe, I take from a most excellent work on this subject, published by Harper & Brothers, entitled, "The Opium Habit." The extracts from Coleridge's letters should have had the same credit :—

WILLIAM WILBERFORCE.

So little is known, beyond what appears in the following brief notices, of the opium habits of this distinguished philanthrophist, that their citation here would be of little service to opium eaters, except as they tend to show that the regular use of the drug in small quantities may sometimes be continued for many years without apparent injury to the health, while the same difficulty in abandoning it is experienced as attends its disuse by those whose moderation has been less marked.

The son of Wilberforce, in the "Life" of his distinguished father, says : "So sparing was he always in its use, that as a stimulant he never knew its power, and as a remedy for his specific weakness he had not to increase its quantity during the last twenty years he lived. 'If I take,' he would often say, 'but a single glass of wine, I

can feel its effect, but I never know when I have taken my
dose of opium by my feelings.' Its intermission was too
soon perceived by the recurrence of disorder."

In a letter from Dr. Gilman, quoted in "The Reminiscences of Coleridge," he says, speaking of the difficulty of
leaving off opium, "I had heard of the failure of Mr.
Wilberforce's case under an eminent physician of Bath."

— :o:—

A HALF CENTURY'S USE OF OPIUM.

The case of Wilberforce, however, is thrown into the
shade by that of a gentleman living in New York — a half
century's use of opium being credited to him — and however this isolated exception to the ordinary results of the
opium habit may be perverted as a snare and delusion to
others, it cannot honestly remain untold. . . . This
gentleman, now in the one hundred and third year of his
age . . . illustrates, as almost a solitary exception,
the fact that a use of opium for half a century, varying in
quantity from forty grains daily to many times this amount,
does not inevitably impair bodily health, mental vigor, or
the higher qualities of the moral nature. . . . In an
endeavor, however, to break up the habit, he was unsuccessful, and the case remains as a striking illustration of
the weakness of that physiological reasoning which would
deduce certain phenomena as the invariable consequences
of a violation of the fundamental laws of health. Until
the chemistry of the living body is better understood,
medical science seems obliged to accept many anomalies
which it cannot explain. About all that can be said of
such an exceptional case is this: In the great conflagra-
tions which at times devastate large cities, some huge
mass of solid masonry is occasionally seen in the midst of
the widespread ruin, looking down upon prostrate columns,
broken capitals, shattered walls, and the cinders and ashes
of a general desolation. The solitary tower unquestiona-
bly stands; but its chief utility lies in this, that it serves

as a striking monument of the appalling and widespread destruction to which it is the sole and conspicuous exception.

***

The question of the permanency of the "overcoming" of the morphine habit in the subjoined narrative is entertained with regret by the compiler of the article. The article in its entirety reads like one who had made heroic struggle for enfranchisement, but again prostrates himself before the "dark idol" in utter hopelessness. My object in incorporating the few selections borrowed, however, is for a far different end,—that he who runs may read the unmistakable evidences of the doom that awaits the intending neophytes in morphia's use, for it should be well understood that no one continues an opium eater from choice. He says in part :—

A MORPHINE HABIT OVERCOME.

"But after a few hours' deprivation of the drug it gave rise to a physical and mental prostration that no pen can adequately depict, no language convey; a horror unspeakable, a woe unutterable takes possession of the entire being; a clammy perspiration bedews the surface, the eye is stony and hard, the nose pointed, as in the Hippocratic face preceding dissolution, the hands uncertain, the mind restless, the heart as ashes, the 'bones marrowless.'

"To the opium consumer, when deprived of this stimulant, there is nothing that life can bestow, not a blessing that man can receive, which would not come to him unheeded, undesired, and be a curse to him. There is but one all-absorbing want, one engrossing desire — his whole being has but one tongue — that tongue syllables but one word — Morphia. And oh! the vain, vain attempt to break this bondage, the labor worse than useless — a minnow struggling to break the toils that bind a Triton !

"I pass over all the horrible physical accompaniments. Suffice it to say that the tongue feels like a copper bolt, and the winding of a watch I have regarded as a task of great magnitude when not under the opium influence, and I was no more capable of controlling, under this condition, the cravings of the system for its pabulum, by any exertion of the will, than I, or any one else, could control the dilatation and contraction of the pupils of the eye under the varying conditions of light and darkness. A time arrives when the will is killed absolutely and literally, and at this period you might, with as much reason, tell a man to will not to die under a mortal disease as to resist the call that his whole being makes, in spite of him, for the pabulum on which it has so long been depending for carrying on its work.

"When you can with reason ask a man to aerate his lungs with his head submerged in water — when you can expect him to control the movements of his limbs while you apply an electric current to its motor nerve — then, but not till then, speak to a confirmed opium eater of 'exerting his will;' reproach him with want of 'determination,' and complacently say to him, 'Cast it from you and bear the torture for a time.' Tell him, too, at the same time, to 'do without atmospheric air, to regulate the reflex action of his nervous system and control the pulsations of his heart.' Tell the Ethiopian to change his skin, but do not mock the misery and increase the agony of a man who has taken opium for years by talking to him of 'will.' Let it be understood that after a certain time (varying, of course, according to the capability of physical resistance, mode of life, etc., of the individual) the craving for opium is beyond the domain of the will. So intolerant is the system under a protracted deprivation, that I know of two suicides resulting therefrom. They were cases of Chinese who were under confinement. They were baffled on one occasion in carrying out a previously successful device for obtaining the drug. The awful mystery of death which they rashly solved had no terrors for them equal to a life without opium, and the morning found them hanging in their cells, glad to get 'anywhere, anywhere out of the world.'

"I attained a daily dose of forty grains, and on more than one occasion I have consumed sixty. It became my bane and antidote; with it I was an *unnatural*—without it, less than man. Food, for months previous to the time of my attaining to such a dose became literally loathsome; its sight would sicken me; my muscles, hitherto firm and well defined, began to diminish in bulk and to lose their contour; my face looked like a hatchet covered with yellow ochre: and this is the best and truest comparison I can institute. It was sharp, fore-shortened and indescribably yellow. I had been taking morphia for nearly two years. . . . Still, I had to keep storing it up in me, trying to extract vivacity, energy, life itself, from that which was killing me; and grudgingly it gave it. I tried hard to free myself, tried, again and again; but I never could at any time sustain the struggle for more than four days at the utmost. At the end of that time I had to yield to my tormentor—yield, broken, baffled and dismayed —yield to go through the whole struggle over again; forced to poison myself—forced with my own hand to shut the door against hope. With an almost superhuman effort I roused myself to the determination of doing something, of making one last effort, and, if I failed, to look my fate in the face. What, thought I, was to be the end of all the hopes I once cherished, and which were cherished of and for me by others? of what avail all the learning I had stored up, all the aspirations I nourished?—all being buried in a grave dug by my own hand, and laid aside like funeral trappings, out of sight and memory. . . . Let it suffice that I fought a desperate fight. Again and again I recoiled, baffled and disheartened; but one aim led me on, and I have come out of the melée bruised and broken it may be, but conquering. One month I waged the fight, and I have now been nearly two without looking at the drug. . . . This it is to be an opium eater; and the boldest may well quail at the picture, drawn not by the hand of fancy, but by one who has supped of its horrors to the full, and who has found that the staff on which he leaned has proven a spear which has wellnigh pierced him to the heart. Let no man believe he will escape : the bond matures at last !"

***

That which follows harmonizes so completely with the narrative above quoted in regard to the "bruised and broken" and shattered physical and mental forces, that it affords a fitting companion picture to the above case. It is intended to convey the results obtained by a gradual reduction of the quantity used, until abandonment of the drug has taken place. The picture is drawn in the emphatic language of Fitz Hugh Ludlow, although I find it doing duty for one of those emancipation (?) allurements held out to inebriates and opium eaters, and reads thus :—

LIQUOR AND OPIUM COMPARED.

"Inebriates have been repeatedly known to risk imminent death if they could not reach their liquor in any other way. The grasp with which liquor holds a man when it turns on him, even after he has abused it for a life-time, compared with the ascendency possessed by opium over the unfortunate habituated to it but for a single year, is as the clutch of an angry woman to the embrace of Victor Hugo's 'Picuvre.' A patient whom, after habitual use of opium for ten years, I met when he had spent eight years more in reducing his daily dose to half a grain of morphia, with a view to its eventual complete abandonment, once spoke to me in these words : 'God seems to help a man in getting out of every difficulty but opium. There you have to claw your way out over red-hot coals on your hands and knees, and drag yourself by main strength through the burning dungeon bars."

To this extract the advertiser of the most prominent "gold cure" in the country, and also for the opium habit, adds: "It is well known that inebriates taken hold of by religious excitement sometimes, for a while, and perhaps permanently, cease wholly the use of alcohol, and lose at once all desire for it. But who ever heard of a confirmed opium user who had experienced such a cure?"

[The redeemed Opium Eater has no knowledge of, and has less sympathy with, emotional "religious excitement;" but if ten years' use of morphine, chloral, etc., constitutes, in medical parlance, a "confirmed opium user," he has announced the fact to thousands, during the past eleven years, of his emancipation from opium, etc., and attributes his deliverance to a Divine source, and, please God, humbly trusts to convey the same intelligence to millions more, "that they come not into this torment!"]

One who was endeavoring to cure himself by reducing his quantum of crude opium at the rate of one grain each twenty-four hours, writes: "From seventeen grains downward, my torment (for by that word alone can I characterize the pangs I endured) commenced. I could not rest, either lying, sitting or standing. I was compelled to shift my position every moment, and the only thing that relieved me was walking about the country. My sight became weak and dim; the gnawing at my stomach was perpetual. . . . A dull, constant pain took possession of the calves of my legs, and there was a continual jerking motion of the nerves from head to foot. My head ached, my intellect was terribly weakened and confused, and I could not think, talk, read or write. . . . I became unable to walk, and used to lie on the floor and roll about in agony for hours together."

In another case, where a very moderate amount of the drug had been used each day, and that only for a few months, the weakened condition of the body and mind was so great as to make life almost useless to him. He says : "During the time I was leaving off opium I had labored under the impression that the habit once mastered, a speedy restoration to health would follow. I was by no means prepared, therefore, for the almost inappreciable gain in the weeks which succeeded. . . . So exceedingly slow has been the process toward the restoration of a natural condition of the system, that writing now, at the expiration of more than a year since opium was finally abandoned, it seems to me very uncertain when, if ever, this result will be reached. Between four and five months elapsed before I was capable of commanding my attention or controlling the nervous impatience of mind and body. . . . The business I had undertaken required a clear head and average health, and I had neither. My sleep was short and imperfect, rarely exceeding two or three hours. My chest was in constant heat and very sore, while my previous bilious difficulties seemed in no way overcome. My mouth was parched, the tongue swollen and a low fever seemed to have taken entire possession of the system, with special and peculiar exasperations in the muscles of the arms and legs. . . . I would sit for hours looking listlessly upon a sheet of paper, helpless of originating an idea upon the commonest of subjects, and with a prevailing sensation of owning a large emptiness in the brain, which seemed filled with a stupid wonder when all this would end. . . . More than an entire year has now passed, in which I have done little less than to put the preceding details into shape from brief memoranda made at the time of the experiment. . . . Had some virus been transfused into the blood, which carried with it to every nerve of sensation a sense of painful, exasperating unnaturalness, the feeling would not, I imagine, be unlike what I am endeavoring to indicate."

"The great majority of those who try this terrible backward path soon turn, affrighted, from its horrors, and go forward toward the ruin that awaits them. But very few who, by reason of extraordinary strength of constitution and will, go through the ordeal and emerge with life and reason, are but wrecks of what they once were. As they lay, like souls in the burning flames of ancient superstition, waiting for the period of their torment to end, they hoped that when, at last, the brazen gate opened and they went out free, they would come into the old, bright world which existed for them before they passed into the eclipse of the drug. They hoped to be strong and full of energy once more. But these hopes are not fulfilled.

"But it is unnecessary to dwell upon the physical agonies of those who try to retrace their steps along the path of the opium habit. The way is paved with red-hot coals and encompassed with burning flames. In addition to the pangs of body there is a distress of mind which broods over like a dense cloud of despair. Whether the victim was sinful, weak, or only deceived makes no difference — the punishment is superlative, surpassing all other pains."

***

The following incidents are from a work published by G. P. Putnam's Sons, New York, entitled "Notes on the Opium Habit." They are the writings of a physician, and may readily find duplications out of the professional experience of many a reputable disciple of Æsculapius. The opinion is expressed by this writer that "the opium habit is, almost invariably, charged by the habitué upon some physician.' The Opium Eater's experience, however, con-

firms him in the fact that the victims of opiates themselves
are the greatest proselyters to this vast army of the
damned, that the works of the flesh, which St. Paul sets
forth in Gal. v. 19, may find greater expression under the
stimulus of drugs, and, further, that the innocent and ignorant, but misguided victim may be the more readily duped
and enslaved by the devotees of lust.   He says, in part :—

"The opium habit is, almost invariably, charged by the
habitué upon some physician who once prescribed an anodyne to relieve pain.

"Thirty years ago, a famous belle, much admired, took
morphine occasionally 'to make her bright when she went
to a party.'

"In after years she took the drug when her children
were sick, because she 'wanted courage — wanted to be
strong.'   As she had eight children, it may be presumed
that in the natural course of events, with so large a family,
she became somewhat accustomed to the use of morphine.
However, she declares that she did not then used it habitually.

"Fourteen years since, at the birth of her youngest
child, she suffered greatly, and her attending physician administered a potion which not only brought relief of pain,
but entranced her senses with visions of rare beauty and
delight.

"'Doctor, what did you give me?' said she.

"Chlorodyne, madame,' replied the doctor.

"'That,' said she to me, 'was a dreadful mistake ; the
doctor ought never, never to have told me.'

"From that time   .   .   .   her one purpose in life was
to obtain chlorodyne, and her occupation to dream away
the hours which intervened between one draught and that
which followed it."

"Eight years since, a bright young lady living in a

country place had a severe attack of neuralgia.   A physician, who was called, left a prescription which relieved her of pains and gave her a good's night rest.

"The following night she repeated the dose on her own account, and this she continued to do, renewing the prescription as she had occasion.   At length her mother, discovering that the little black vial was making frequent trips to the drug store, requested a translation of the prescription.

"'It's only laudanum, madam,' said the apothecary.

"'She then endeavored to have it discontinued; but it was too late, and for more than seven years this unfortunate girl was a most unhappy victim, becoming a nervous, hysterical, permaturely old young lady, breaking her mother's heart and sending her sorrowing to the grave.

"None but those who have made a study of the subject have any conception of the potent influence of this drug.

"Physicians who are accustomed to prescribe narcotics daily, and who do not know, perhaps, of a single instance where harm has resulted, are apt to be incredulous when told of the prevalence of this habit.   .   .   .   Still, when we consider the number of medical Ishmaelites throughout the country living on their gains gathered by the sale of 'antidotes' to this class of people, many of whom have spent their money before they seek a cure, we must conclude that the evil is widespread.

"It is frequently asked how one can form such a habit secretly; why it is so rarely discoverved until too late to stop it.   .   .   .   A gentleman called on me recently to arrange for the treatment of his wife, for what she called 'a nervous complaint.'   She confessed to me privately that the actual trouble was two bottles of morphine per week, and begged me not to let her husband know it.

"Since I have given special attention to this subject, persons have come to me, secretly addicted to the habit, whom I should not have suspected.   Some conceal it, for a considerable time, from their nearest friends.   Many women are taking the drug today without the knowledge of husband or family.

"Some day the package of morphine — purchased in a neighboring city, and addressed in a fictitious name, but whose real destination is well known to the little clerk in the post office — will fall into the hands of her busy, absent-minded husband, and then everybody will be surprised — some that she concealed the habit so long, and some that no one but herself ever suspected it!

"The first prescription truly 'acts like a charm' upon the distressed patient, whose nervous system is impaired. He well remembers how it smoothed his pillow, changed the hard bed beneath him to softest down, closed his weary eyelids, and whispered dreams of contentment and peace. But the enchantress is now changed to a dragon which holds him under a magic spell. During the brief period of exhilaration, when in dreamy revery, with half-closed eye, he looks listlessly out upon the world, it seems easy to throw off the spell which binds him, and he proposes to do so—but not just now. He is not quite ready.

"At length the time comes when, spurred to a supreme effort by the pressure of circumstances — the taunt of friend or foe, or by the earnest pleading of wife or child— he resolves to be free from bondage to a degrading appetite. To give strength for thought, reflection, and plan of action, an extra portion is taken. Under its influence he is brave and resolute. He now determines to reform, or die in the attempt. Soon, however, he becomes dispirited, depressed, anxious. If he persists and allows the time to pass without his daily dose, a feeling of great distress takes possession of him. He falls asleep, but frightful dreams quickly waken him, trembling and crying out in terror. The judgment has come, and the Evil One is reaching out his great brown hand to seize him! Time seems to stand still. He stares at the clock, saying : 'Are there sixty minutes in an hour? No, there are sixty hours in every minute!' At one moment he is burning up,—

then he shivers with cold.   Perspiration streams from
every pore.   Neuralgic pains torture successively his head,
limbs, joints, arms, chest and back.   Indeed, every nerve
of the body seems to cry out, and nerves are discovered
where none were known to him before.   A peculiar, indescribable sensation, more severe than actual pain, torments
him from head to foot.   Obstinate vomiting sets in, followed by persistent, exhaustive diarrhœa.

"Finally, in deep humiliation, in anguish and tears, he
gives up the attempt, and bows in subjection to his merci-
less master."

.

In closing this line of evidence, I again quote from the
admirable article by Fitz Hugh Ludlow, and which appeared in Harper's Magazine for August, 1867, entitled
"What Shall They Do to Be Saved?"   If the redeemed
Opium Eater errs not, this gentleman was at the head of
an institution for opium eaters located on Lord's Island.   I
recall with painful recollection my pathetic appeal to a
moneyed friend for the means of making one more effort
for liberty.   But, alas! to this day it has remained un-
noticed.   Its indorsement by Rev. Henry Ward Beecher
was the stimulus that brightened my hopes, but poverty's
blighting and withering shadow doomed me to disappoint-
ment.   I have, however, since met a gentleman who had
been under treatment there for the cocaine, as well as the
morphine, habit.   He was himself a druggist; had spent
thousands of dollars in a vain attempt to find relief.   In a
long interview with him, I extract this thought expressed
by him, "I believe I am in this hell for no other reason
than that I have been the means of putting so many others
there before me!"   The prolific source of knowledge thus
afforded Dr. Ludlow, makes his article on this theme very

instructive reading to the student on the opium habit. His final diagnosis of a confirmed and hopeless case of opium using reads in part thus :—

"The result of our consultation was a unanimous agreement not to press the case further. Physicians have no business to consider the speculative question, whether death without opium is preferable to life with it. They are called to keep people on the earth. We were convinced that to deprive the patient longer of opium would be to kill him. This we had no right to do without his consent. He did not consent. . . .

"He will have to take opium all his life. Further struggle is suicide. Death will probably occur at any rate not from an attack of what we usually consider disease, but from the disintegrating effects on tissue of the habit itself. So, whatever he may do, his organs march on to death. He will have to continue the habit which kills him only because abandoning it kills him sooner ; for self-murder has dropped out of the purview of the moral faculties and become a mere animal question of time. The only way left him to preserve his intellectual faculties intact is to keep his future daily dose at the tolerable minimum. Henceforth all his dreams of entire liberty must be relegated to the world to come. He may be valuable as a monitor, but in the executive uses of this mighty modern world henceforth he can never share. Could the immortal soul find itself in a more inextricable, a more 'grisly' complication ?" . . .

After accurately and minutely portraying the various stages in the opium eater's physical decay, he closes his graphic picture in the following language :—

"The rest of your life must be spent in keeping comfortable, not in being happy."

"Opium eaters enjoy a strange immunity from other

diseases. They are not liable to be attacked by miasma in malarious countries; epidemics or contagions where they exist. They almost always survive to die of their opium itself. And an opium death is usually in one of these two manners :—

"The opium eater either dies in collapse through nervous exhaustion (with the blood-poisoning and delirium above mentioned), sometimes after an overdose, but oftener seeming to occur spontaneously; or in the midst of physical or mental agony so great and irrelievable as men suffer in hopeful abandonment of the drug, and with a colliquative diarrhœa, by which — in a continual fiery, acrid discharge — the system relieves itself during a final fortnight of the effete matters which have been accumulating for years.

"Either of these ends is terrible enough. Let us draw a curtain over their details.

"Opium is a corrosion and paralysis of all the noblest forms of life. The man who voluntarily addicts himself to it, would commit in cutting his throat a suicide only swifter and less ignoble.

"The habit is gaining fearful ground among our professional men, the operatives in our mills, our weary sewing-women, our fagged clerks, our disappointed wives, our former liquor-drunkards, our very day-laborers, who a generation ago took gin. All our classes, from the highest to the lowest, are yearly increasing their consumption of the drug. The terrible demands, especially in this country, made on modern brains by our feverish competitive life, constitute hourly temptations to some form of the sweet, deadly sedative. Many a professional man of my acquaintance, who twenty years ago was content with his *tri-diurnal* 'whiskey,' ten years ago, drop by drop, began taking stronger 'laudanum cock-tails,' until he became what he is now — an habitual opium eater. I have tried to show what he will be. If this article shall deter any from an imitation of his example, or excite an interest in the question—'What he shall do to be saved?'—I am content."

"Over the opium eater's coffin at least, thank God, a wife and a sister can stop weeping and say, 'He's free!'"

* *
*

MORPHINE VS. ALCOHOLIC STIMULATION.

"What is the stimulating effect of morphia? Does it make one intoxicated like liquor?" the writer of these "Confessions" has often been asked.

Drunk or intoxicated? No, I answer. The effect is entirely dissimilar from that of intoxicating beverages. Liquor, even in my early indulgencies, never gave to me that lightness and exuberance of spirit usually witnessed in the early votaries of alcoholic stimulants. It never created false hopes, but rather revealed the true character of my nature, and enabled me to face mortifying scenes or bridge over weaknesses I felt unable to carry without it. It gave me the courage to tell a disagreeable truth about myself, where otherwise I would have resorted to evasion. Morphine "braced up" to the highest tension the fearful spirit, and carried me through scenes which mortification and shame would have left me incapable of performing. It produced in an already hopeless and abandoned nature the power of strengthening it to walk publicly where solitude and retirement would have otherwise been chosen. In the last years of its use, when badly overcome by intoxicating liquors, a recourse to morphia combatted largely the intoxicating influence produced by the alcoholic stimulant. I recall times when, recognizing the fact that I had drunk to the verge of incapacity, I have resorted to morphine, and it has overthrown the momentary effects of the liquor.

Morphia's influence upon the soul might be likened to one who had suddenly become intoxicated or entranced by beauty or by music, or some grand theme or scene that thrills the soul, and, for lack of language, no expression of its sublimity can be given by the enchanted mind.   They desire not to break in or mar their happiness by vulgar expression.   They drink silently and alone; none but themselves are conscious of their joy and happiness.   To give expression to it would rob one's self of it.

Thus, for instance, opium, like wine, gives an expansion to the heart and the benevolent affection, but with this remarkable difference, that in the sudden development of kind-heartedness which accompanies inebriation, there is always more or less of a maudlin character which exposes it to the contempt of the bystanders.   Men shake hands, swear eternal friendship, and shed tears, — no mortal knows why,— and the low sensuality of human nature is clearly uppermost.   But the expansion of the benignant feelings incident to morphia is no febrile access, but a healthy restoration to that state to which the mind would naturally recover upon the removal of any deep-seated irritation of pain that had disturbed and quarreled with the impulses of a heart originally good and just.   Wine stimulation leads a man to the brink of absurdity and extravagance, and beyond a certain point it is sure to volatilize and to disperse the intellectual energies; whereas morphine always seems to compose what had been agitated, and to concentrate what had been distracted.   In short, to sum up all in a few words, a man who is inebriated or tending to inebriation, is, and feels that he is, in a condition which calls up into supremacy the merely human, too

(I speak as one who was not suffering from any disease)
often the brutal, part of his nature; but the opium eater
feels that the diviner part of his nature is paramount;
that is, the moral affections are in a state of cloudless
serenity; and over all is the great light of a majestic
intellect.

The above is very De Quincey-ish, and is almost a ver-
batim description by him of wine and laudanum stimulation.   The picture is incomplete, however, until there is
hung by its side Agony, gathered from all things natural
as well as infernal, as an inviting sequence to the ethereal
realms of bliss found by him in opium.

Morphia! thou art the incarnation of him who dragged
from heavenly bliss the mighty host of foolish virgins!—
thy name Lucifer! the bright the Morning Star!   And
thy abode, where Hope has fled, and Despair sits triumphant in its stead!   O subtle drug!   May thy mighty
power lose weight in Intelligence Divine!

***

GOVERNMENT RESPONSIBILITY IN THE OPIUM TRAFFIC.

The following information in regard to Government responsibility in the opium traffic is from the New York
World of several years ago.   It is "borrowed" simply
to give a general idea of the subject and history on this
important matter.   Statistically it is not up to date, it being generally conceded that China alone has 300,000,000,
or 70 per cent, of her population enthralled in the opium
curse.   It says:—

More than 100,000,000 of China are directly or indirectly, suffering from the use of opium.   The writer of

the article on opium in the last edition of Encyclopædia
Britannica, states the number of those who use it to
be 100,000,000 or 125,000,000, as the population may be
300,000,000 or 400,000,000.

And now the British Government in India, to increase
its revenue, has authorized the licensing of shops throughout India and Burmah for the free sale of opium.   These
licenses are issued in a very unusual form.   Those who
take the license come under obligation to sell a stipulated
amount or pay a forfeit!   Thus the Government almost
compels the holders of the license to stimulate its subjects
to consume a deadly poison.   The door is thrown wide
open for all the inhabitants of India to take that which
destroys at once the body and the soul.

The unrestricted sale of opium is permitted in Java, with
its 20,000,000 of population.   It is also permitted in the
French possessions in Southeastern Asia, with a population of 8,000,000 or 10,000,000.   The vice is also carried
by the Chinese immigrants into Siam and all the islands
of the Eastern Archipelago.   If the populations of the
various countries in Asia in which the free sale of opium
is permitted are added together, the aggregate number is
more than 600,000,000!

The laws of China once prohibited the sale and use of
opium, the violation of which was punished by death.   So
earnest were the Chinese to prevent its introduction into
the country, that the Government became involved in a
costly war with England about it, at the close of which a
treaty was made in which England recognized China's
right to prohibit the introduction of opium, but left it
with China to seize the vessels that smuggled it in and
confiscate the vessel and cargo!   But as the smugglers
were Englishmen and the ships English ships, the Chinese
were afraid to execute the law, and so opium was brought
in English bottoms from India to China from 1842 to
1860.   After thus fighting the traffic for sixty years, the
Chinese Government, finding it could not stop the smug-

gling of opium into the country by British vessels, finally
gave up the contest, and submitted to legalize the horrible
traffic which it could not destroy.   And once admitting it
into the country it could not enforce the laws against its
sale and use, and shops were opened in every city, town and
village in the empire.   The next step was, as they could
not keep out the opium from India, to begin the cultivation
of the poppy in China itself.   Now the opium made from
the native-grown poppy is said to be three times as much
in quantity as that imported from India.

In the districts where it is thus grown the price of the
native opium is very cheap, and its consumption has
spread among men, women and children, so that some resident missionaries in these districts say that sixty and seventy out of every hundred of the people are more or less
opium eaters.   When I went to China in 1844, it was supposed that 2,000,000 used it.   Before I left China I estimated that the 2,000,000 had grown to 40,000,000, while
Hudson Taylor now puts the number of those who use it,
directly or indirectly, at 100,000,000.

Now let us sum up the enormous extent of this curse.
The population of India and Burmah, according to the
census taken in 1880, was 285,000,000 ; that of China is
350,000,000 — some make it 400,000,000.   The Island of
Java counts its 20,000,000, to which the French possessions in Southeastern Asia add at least 10,000,000 more.
The Eastern Archipelago has say 5,000,000, making altogether a total of 670,000,000.   The curse of Asia has
been saddled upon that continent by Christian Europe.
For this terrible blight cast upon the greatest of the four
quarters of the globe the British Government is chiefly
responsible.   A hundred years ago the East India Company commenced to monopolize the production of opium
for sale in China, and the Government at home gave to
the company the protection of the British flag.   Since
1858 the British Government has had a monopoly of the
production and sale of opium.   Great Britain is thus di-

rectly responsible for the prevalence of the opium plague among the 670,000,000 people in Asia."

A melancholy report comes from the Marquesas and other French islands in the South Pacific. It is to the effect that the natives of those islands are becoming exterminated by opium. Mr. W. Hoffner, formerly manager of the French Commercial Company there, says of them: "The natives are dying off like flies. In ten years, if the present rate of mortality keeps up, there will not be one of them left." The French Government itself introduced opium to the natives twenty years ago, and the present deplorable state of affairs is therefore directly due to France. Now the authorities are trying to stop the deadly traffic, but in vain. When a whole race becomes so depraved, deteriorated, and dirty that it is a menace to the rest of mankind, nature summarily snuffs it out, as she is doing with the Marquesas and Dominique islanders now. But what should be said of the civilized French nation, that anticipated and upset nature by destroying with opium a fine, strong race of savages, who might have become a credit to civilization, just as the new style of Indian will be in America?

* *

DR. KEELEY ON THE OPUIM HABIT.

That which follows is from a work devoted to advertising Dr. Leslie E. Keeley's "Double Chloride of Gold" for the morphine habit. The man and the remedy were both known to the opium eaters of the country many years ago by a minute advertisement calling attention to his medicine for the morphine habit. "It was weighed in the balance and found wanting" by three of the redeemed Opium Eater's unfortunate morphine victim acquaintances, who, haply, have since found emancipation in death. That the

distinguished practitioner can speak authoritatively as to
opium's victims, is my only reason for incorporating the
subjoined extracts from his book entitled " The Fetters
Broken ":—

Thirty years ago the quantity of opium imported into the
United States was 109,526 pounds.   The first importation
of morphia occurred the same year, and consisted of but
twelve ounces.   In 1871, ten years later, the import of the
drug was 315,121 pounds, and of morphia 237 ounces.   In
1880, the opium imported was 533,451 pounds, and 8,822
ounces of morphia were received at the port of New York.
Add to these figures about ten per cent for smuggled
opium, and we have some idea of the quantity then used
in the United States.   A comparison between 1861 and
1871 shows a fearful increase in ten years, yet the difference between 1871 and 1880 shows a still larger increase
in nine years.   The revenue statistics unmistakably show
that the consumption of opium is rapidly increasing, and
that, too, far in excess of the increase of population.   In
1880 this country received 97,000 pounds of opium from
China, 326,975 from England, and 92,633 from Turkey in
Asia.   The crude opium after reaching this country un-
dergoes different processes at the hands of manufacturers,
a large portion of it being made into the sulphate of morphia.   In 1876 it was estimated that there were 225,000
opium users in this country, at least two-thirds of them
belonging to the better classes of society.   Today it is
estimated that there are not less than one and one-half
million.

One and one-half million men and women in America
slaves of a drug!   The thought of slavery is in itself ab-
horrent ; but when we remember that this is a slavery the
most damnable on earth ; a bondage to a soulless, merci-
less tyrant ; a captivity whose daylight is Despair and
whose Hope is Death,—the impressive fact fills our minds

with pity and sympathy! It will thus be seen that on an average three in every hundred are slaves to the drug in some form. The saddest feature of this is that the majority of the victims are women. Not poor, degraded, outcast women,—although this class helps to swell the list,—but those occupying high positions in the world. Brilliant society ladies, zealous workers in good causes, literary toilers, ambitious women, have fallen beneath the witching power of morphia. The simple fact that women form by far the larger proportion of those using the drug is one that should excite universal pity ; the more so as they are not generally responsible for contracting the habit.

Some localities have a greater proportion than others, the South having more victims than the North, and the city more than the country. Texas is said to have more opium users in proportion to its population than any State in the Union, and I believe the claim to be well founded. The effects of the war upon the South were very marked in this matter, as since that time the habit has largely increased in the Southern States. In Albany, New York, there is annually consumed 3,500 pounds of opium, 5,500 ounces of morphia, and about 500,000 pills of morphine. In Chicago, Ill., there are about 25,000 persons addicted to the morphine habit, and the leading druggists, according to a recent statement, say that their principal customers are ladies. In St. Louis, Mo., it is estimated that there are not less than 20,000, while many Southern cities show, in proportion to population, even higher figures than these. I know small towns where the average is five in every hundred, and the habit is constantly increasing.

The amount annually paid out for the drug by these victims is about $15,000,000 : an immense sum, which is deflected from the proper channels of industry and commerce, and devoted to a vice which is destructive to both soul and body, and detrimental to the best interests of mankind and of society.

Three grains of morphine will, as a general rule, cause

death.   This fact is not generally known to those unac-
quainted with the properties of morphine, but it ought to
be well understood by everybody.   Our high schools ought
to teach this fact, and also the greater truth, that when
a man can so accustom his system to the use of a poison
in doses more than sufficient to cause death in ordinary
cases, he subjects his system to abnormal effects which
must have a disastrous, and in time a deadly, influence
upon the mind and the body. .   .   .

Fifty years ago, gum opium was used exclusively by
those addicted to the drug, but morphine has largely su-
perseded the original juice of the poppy.   The majority of
those using drugs now employ the sulphate of morphia,
chiefly because of its potency (it being six times stronger
than the gum opium), its small bulk, and the rapidity with
which it affects the system.   It has been stated that the
greater proportion inject the solution subcutaneously by
means of the hypodermic syringe, and my experience leads
me to believe that this class predominates.

If it were possible to paint all the horrors, the agonies,
and woes which this deceitful drug has wrought upon humanity, it would form a picture of unparalleled misery
and despair.   The mere recital of figures and the facts
which they teach will, however, be sufficient to stir up a
spirit of inquiry and investigation.   They are sufficiently
startling to cause alarm, and lead us to seek some explanation of so dire a curse, and some method for stopping its
sweeping ravages.

The above should have been credited to Dr. Leslie E.
Keeley's (of Dwight, Ill.) earlier pamphlet, issued in 1883,
entitled "The Morphine User," and hence is not up to
date statistically; but to the mind given in this direction,
sufficient has been revealed in the figures to make a good
foundation for approximating the victims of the opium
habit of the United States.   Dr. Keeley, in his more re-

cent publication, has a chapter on cocaine. I have inci-
dentally referred in these pages to a druggist who was
dually afflicted with the morphine and cocaine habits. " I
use cocaine," said this unfortunate man, "because of the
quick relief afforded me." He had unsuccessfully sought
relief from his direful state. Dr. Keeley says of this
drug :—

THE COCAINE HABIT.

When cocaine was first brought to the notice of the profession, the new anæsthetic was heralded from one end of
the world to the other. Lauded in medical journals and
by the press, by those interested in its sale and production, physicians recommended it, after superficial investigation, innocently, perhaps, but with fatal ignorance of its
dangers. The opium habitués used it, and its first effect
seemed to warrant its being vaunted as a cure. The professional spread the glad tidings, which were taken up by
the newspapers and echoed and re-echoed as the long-
sought-for "way of escape." And so the poor victim went
from bad to worse, owning in consequence a dual slavery.
Gladly would he retrace his steps and escape the relentless pursuit of a double Nemesis.

The history of this drug is a short one ; but in its tendency to sap every interest in life, to destroy every noble
ambition, to subvert manhood and uproot all obligations to
God and family, it stands at the head as the most hurtful
and devilish in its power for evil of all the drugs for which
a habit can be formed ; degrading as it does, man — that
noblest of all God's creatures, which He endowed with
His own image and likeness — to an object of loathing and
disgust to himself, and of humiliation to his friends. So
benign is its influence, few suspect the lurking demon hidden within or heed the prophetic warning, "In the day
thou eatest thereof thou shalt surely die." Alluring and

fascinating in its balmy atmosphere of serenity and pleasure, like the treacherous mirage, it tempts the unwary traveler with pictures of Elysian fields and flowing fountains, only to leave him at last in a trackless desert, a prey to those jackals of the profession, unprincipled traffickers in the woes of humanity.

Used originally as a local anæsthetic, no fears of constitutional effects were entertained. Experience proving it cumulative, a small dose will usually effect a system once under its influence as much as a larger dose of opium.

To obviate the depression which follows its use, and silence the reproaches of a still sensitive conscience, the victim resorts to the drug again and again for its exhilarating effects rather than as a relief from pain. Its distinctive feature is due to hyperemia of the nerve centers ; but as the effect is only transient, reaction sets in with ever increasing power and with lessening intervals, until the habit is formed.

I have no desire to make the famous doctor "an offender for a word," yet I am glad to record the fact that in cocaine he recognizes that by the simple law of repeated indulgence "the habit is formed," and unlike alcoholic stimulants and morphia it is not a disease!

There are pre-natal tendencies, hereditary taints and pasions, and there are also ACQUIRED habits and passions, —latent forces which spring into being by contact and continual environment.

DRUGS USED IN ATTEMPTS TO CURE.

The late Dr. Albert Day, for many years superintendent of the Washingtonian Home for inebriates, located at Boston, and a life-long student of inebriety and advocate of temperance, in several cordial interviews with him, the redeemed Opium Eater sat at the feet of this Gamaliel with a life-long practice in "straightening out" the debauchees from alcoholic drunkenness, and he stigmatized (to borrow Dr. Keeley's expression) as "jackals of the profession" and "unprincipled traffickers in the woes of humanity," those who claimed to have found "cures" for drunkenness. He told me, in substance, the same that I understand from reading Dr. Keeley's works, that the only recourse left is the administration of poisons more powerful than those contained in alcoholic liquors. We never pretend to cut out the hidden ulcers of his moral nature, but from the treatment and care that he receives, the forces of life again assert themselves. A man on a "spree" is like a ship in a furious gale; like her, he becomes dismantled and dismasted, loses chart and compass, and drifts about in abandonment and uselessness. To save the ship, reclaim her to future usefulness, provisions have been made in civilized ports. Man has made the same endeavor for his stranded and fallen fellow-man in homes and sanitoriums, where by kind care and medical treatment—like the ship remantled and remasted — he is again fitted to go forth; but he must again encounter the hurricane and the cyclone of his physical and moral nature in his daily and hourly mingling among men in the swift current of human affairs, and do battle with the same invisible powers that lays siege for his soul in the intense cravings of his being for alcoholic stimulation. We cannot cure; we only mend. But as in the knitting together of the disunited bones, let us hope that the lessons derived from drinking "cures" may heal and knit together the bruised parts, that God-given intelligence and power will enable us poor, dwarfed humanity to try and do something for ourselves.

In that which follows, Dr. Keeley is in criticism on some one of the many "unprincipled traffickers in the woes of humanity" who has resorted to the same method — subcutaneous injections of powerful poisons — in the "cure" of the opium habit, as the doctor makes use of in the cure of the alcoholic "disease." He says of the effect of one of these poisons thus used :—

Atropia is simply a poison, and one of the most deadly poisons known to man. It has no power to heal. It is a minister of death — not of life. It cannot cure the opium habit in any proper sense of the word. The opium user to whom it is administered can be "sustained" by much less than his usual daily "ration" of opium or morphine, I admit ; but it is simply a case of one poison being over-mastered by another more powerful. The strong man is driven from his citadel by one stronger than he. The whole system is so utterly benumbed by atropia that it cannot, for the time being, realize the morphine crave. But there is no tonic or sedative virtue in this deadly drug. If it be possible for a victim of the opium habit to finally abandon the drug under atropia treatment, his last stage will be worse than the first. His nervous system, bruised and beaten down by the trampling feet of the two gigantic demons in their conflict, will feel no thrills of returning health. If any of the organs of his body were disordered, their debilitated condition will be aggravated. If any lesion of the heart is present, the patient will probably die during the atropia treatment. And if, after undergoing treatment by this poison, and being turned off as cured simply because his desire for morphine is temporarily paralyzed by the grip of a stronger poison,— if after this his nerves should begin to recover a little from the influence of the atropia, his craving for opium will spring up with more than its original strength. Such treatment and such cures are worse than the disease itself.

While I do not claim to have verified the incident, yet I am prepared, by my own experiments and observation, to accept as true a telegram sent from Atlanta, Georgia, and widely published, to the effect that the wife of a Baptist clergyman, well-known in the vicinity, was found dead on the train near Atlanta, her death being caused by an over-dose of morphine taken by her as she was returning from treatment in an establishment which advertises to cure the opium habit, and in which the "hypodermic method" and atropia are depended upon. Such "cures" are all that can be expected from such a poison.

This is a serious matter. I have heard of opium users being cured, but have never been able to have them located by my informants. But there have been an innumerable number of instances, on the other hand, where all human aid as failed. Is there no lesson in this for you? There are as many "Thou shalt nots" to be observed today in order that joy and happiness may be ours, as there were Moses gave when them to darkened Israel.

.

The following notes and information have been gathered from various sources, and are interesting from the standpoint of variety. They are largely without credit in many instances, not having in view their insertion in this work.

The poppy is an annual plant, with the stalk rising to the height of three or four feet; its leaves resemble those of the lettuce, and its flower has the appearance of the tulip. When at its full growth an incision is made in the top of the plant, from which there issues a white, milky juice, which soon hardens, and is scraped off the plants, and wrought into cakes. In this state it is protected with the petals of the plant and dried and exported to the countries where it is manufactured into morphia or consumed by the habitué of the smoker of opium.

The raising of opium is a very hazardous business—the poppy being a delicate plant, peculiarly liable to injury from insects, wind, hail or unseasonable rain. The produce seldom agrees with the true average, but commonly runs in extremes; while one cultivator is disappointed, another reaps immense gain. One season does not pay the labor of the culture; another, peculiarly fortunate, enriches all cultivators. This circumstance is well suited to allure man, ever confident of good fortune. [Colebrooke's Husbandry of Bengal.

Opium is produced in various parts of the East Indies, but the principal seat of its culture is along the Ganges, where, in a tract of country about two hundred miles wide by six hundred miles long, in 1872, between 500,000 and 600,000 acres were devoted to the poppy. In some districts the manufacture is under Government control, while in others it is left to private enterprise, the Government collecting an export duty.

Opium is chiefly prepared in India, Turkey, and Persia, but the white poppy is extensively cultivated in France and other parts of Europe, on account of the capsules and of the useful bland oil obtained from its seed. It is also cultivated, and opium made, in England.

The chemical composition of opium is remarkable. The alkaloid morphia, its most valuable constituent, was discovered in 1816 by an apothecary named Serturner, of Hanover, Prussia.

The use of opium as an habitual stimulant, producing exhilaration and pleasant flights of fancy or dreams, is very prevalent in the greater part of the world, our own country being by no means an exception. It is a vice less easy of detection than alcoholic intoxication, which it is said to replace where law and custom have made the latter disreputable. Its evil effects are most manifest upon the nervous and digestive system.

Opium eaters are as particular in regard to the "brand" of the drug they use, as is the most fastidious connoisseur in any article of diet or flavor of cigar, or the alcoholic imbiber for his peculiar stimulant.

Opium is the Mephistopheles of the age! Insidious and deceitful in its character, it has permeated all classes of society with its baleful influence, and in thousands of homes it holds an autocratic sway. The physician daily meets it in some of its Protean forms, for it has defiled the sacred desk, sullied the pure ermine of justice, ruthlessly entered every profession ; nay, fastened its terrible fangs upon every class and condition of our people!

The ancients paid sacred homage to Morpheus, god of sleep and dreams ; and now, in the midst of an age of intelligence and advancement, we find a vast army of men and women bowing at the shrine of the arch-fiend Morphia, named after the classic deity of old!

From a careful estimate by the best authorities, it is believed that tobacco is used by 800,000,000 persons throughout the globe, opium by 400,000,000, and hemp by from 200,000,000 to 300,000,000 souls. Thus about two thirds of the whole human race employ tobacco ; one third, opium ; and one fourth, hemp, as narcotic indulgences. ["Narcotics," North America Review, October, 1862.] I am safe in adding that the ratio has not decreased in the use of narcotics during the past thirty odd years.

Ancient mythology, which symbolized so many things which we now recognize, and drew such clear and just distinctions between many of those relations which are the same in all ages, well designated Sleep, Dreams, and Death as children of Night. Sleep dwelt in Cimmerian darkness, and bore the poppy as his emblem. The god of Dreams was also called Morpheus, from the various images or *forms* seen in such visions. Death was no skeleton among the ancients, but a fair bodily form like the rest, bearing an inverted torch. The use and influence of narcotics seem to vivify for us these old resemblances. Physiology, at any rate, teaches us that their effects are very nearly allied to those of natural dreams.

Dr. P. Hehir, surgeon captain in the Bengal army, has made an extended study of the opium habit. He estimates that there are 1,400,000 consumers in Hyderabad out of a population of 11,000,000. He says that twelve per cent of the Mohammedans, seven per cent of the Hindus, and five per cent of the Pariahs use it. Each devotee on the average consumes eight grains per day—four in the morning, and four in the evening. If used in moderation it enables a person to do more work on less food and sleep than otherwise. For the time being, it gives him unusual cheerfulness and disposition to work, calms irritation, allays excitement, conquers resentment, quiets the nerves and emotions, lengthens life, diminishes the death-rate, cures diabetes,* and never produces organic disease. Its chief evil is producing constipation. Indian opium is pure and contains but little morphine. Life insurance companies charge no extra premium on the lives of opium eaters in India.

---

* The above is incorporated here that its rose-colored tints may be controverted. It is largely true, but that it cures diabetes, or any other disease, is not tenable. Morphine produces on the urinary organs the same effect that it does upon the bowels — it causes retention A patient dying of acute gastritis once said to me, after a morphine injection, "I have no stomach since I took the opium." Nevertheless, the disease was there, although the pain had been alleviated for the time being by the drug. The same holds good with diabetes and all other ills under opium's power.

It is not given to any human being to known the line at which an indulgence becomes a habit.   That line has been crossed by the feet of innumerable millions hastening with laughter and shouting along the first gentle descent of the way of death, but not one of them saw, or could ever tell, just where the fatal point was passed.   They did not look, they did not think, they did not take heed.   The laws which avenge evil indulgences by changing them into tyrannous habits are indeed shod with wool, and do their work with quiet, noiseless hands.   Slowly, unceasingly, "without haste, without rest," the wreaths of flowers are replaced by silken bands, and the bands of silk by chains of steel.   The consciousness of liberty remains long after the bondage has become as fixed and certain as the grasp of Fate.

When I had been taking thirty grains of sulphate of morphia every twenty-four hours for a long time, I got to thinking one day how the drug was utterly ruining my life and killing me by inches, and I resolved firmly for the first time after forming the habit to stop its use.   And for four days I did stop.   But if I had gone without it one day or even a few hours longer I should have been a raving maniac.   No brain could endure such agonies for any longer period.   "Hell tortures" is no name for them !

The love of narcotics is universal.   A survey of the whole world shows that no nation is so poor, barbarous, or obscure as not to have found and adopted its favorite and peculiar luxury of this sort.   The Chinese sink under the soft but adamantine chains of opium ; the races of India, the Persians, and the Turks stimulate the imagination to frenzy with hemp ; other Asiatic nations, as well as the Malays and Pacific Islanders, chew the Betel-nut ; the South American ascends the slopes of the Andes with lighter step and freer breath under the influence of Coca ; the same tribes, as well as some castes in India, make an

intoxicating beverage with the thorn-apple, or Stramonium ;
and even the poor Siberian or Kamtchatkan gratifies his
longing for narcotic indulgences with an humble toadstool,
the Siberian Fungus.   The hop is the narcotic distinctive
of England, coffee the nervous stimulant of France, tea of
Russia, and all three of the United States.   Tobacco is so
common a narcotic, that it is used also by those who resort to more powerful substances of the kind ; and so far
do these soothing habits penetrate unsuspected into our
daily diet, that the dozing matron has her afternoon nap
prolonged, if not occasioned, by a narcotic principle —
Lactucarium — which she absorbs from the lettuce of her
salad.   ["The Seven Sisters of Sleep."   London : James
Blackwood.

The uses of opium in medicine are many.   Besides its
lawful consumption, which is large, opium is used secretly
in patent medicines and quack preparations to an enormous extent.   In point of fact, two drugs form the grand
"stand-bys" of the makers of secret nostrums.   For all
purgatives, laxatives, and liver-regulators, aloes is used.
For all anodyne, anti-spasmodic, anti-neuralgic combina-
tions, for cough mixtures, diarrhœa mixtures, infant car-
minatives, and "soothing syrups," opium, in the form of
morphine, laudanum, or paregoric, is the *sine qua non*.
Other ingredients may vary, but the certain and cheap
narcotic never.   We are sorry to say that those very remedies which are puffed as free from opium or paregoric,
and hence adapted to the tenderest infancy, often contain
large amounts of this drug.   ["Narcotics," North American Review, October, 1862.

There is one relation in which opium deserves all the
praise that the most ardent fancy can heap upon it ; and
that is its relation to sickness and pain.   Here it may indeed be called " the Gift of God."   Sydenham said that
he would not practice medicine without opium ; and no

modern skeptic has been bold enough to exclude it from his barren list of indispensable drugs. No other narcotic is so trustworthy and so sure, in the average of constitutions, to produce sleep, soothe pain, relax painful spasm, and support the vitality under the most terrible strains of severe injury, or the slow drainage of chronic. disease. The multitude who have gone before us, and those over whose thousand sick-beds in civilized land the angel of death is hovering, uncertain where to strike, could they speak, would but repeat the same thanks for the comfortable intervals and the calm nights afforded them in their anguish by this divine benefaction. . . . To the physician who has thus watched its influence it seems certain that this was the only and the unique use for which Providence intended it; and that its imployment as an indulgence by those in health is but a base perversion of its higher power. [North American Review, 1862.

And but for that "base perversion" and its inevitable result are these pages written. This seems a fitting stopping place for this line of my work, and I leave this indispensable minister of pain, trusting and hoping that the experiences herein related may awaken a conscientious investigation of the power and use of this drug on the part of those who are called to a high and holy calling in their ministrations to sick and suffering among humanity — the physician. To the unfortunate sufferer, I would say, bear with heroic fortitude the pain and agony of physical distress, and await that rest which comes from such a battle with nature. It is infinitely more beneficial and lasting than that artificially derived from anodynes in any form, out of which you merge weary and exhausted, with parched and feverish symptoms. In the hour of sad bereavement—the Gethsemane into which we must all enter — turn not nor be turned to Morphia's magic power, but rather look for consolation and hope in the Spirit that sustained Him who was stretched upon Calvary's Cross, and to the inner consciousness of your own soul that reiterates to you that the burden to be borne can only successfully and profitably be done to your own good, when maintained, not by drugs, but in the faith and spirit made manifest in the Carpenter's Son.

*_**

THE OPIUM-SMOKING HABIT.

"How use doth breed a habit in a man."—Shakspeare.

"O death in life!—the days that are no more."—Tennyson.

I am constrained by an irresistible impulse to supplement these "Confessions" with the following pages on the worst type and apparently most degrading form of the opium curse,— opium-smoking. This impulse is not born, however, by an immediate experience — for I feel happy in stating that in "hitting the pipe" I am as yet uninitiated, — notwithstanding, I feel I am as qualified from a personal association and mingling with Chinamen with a view to understanding my theme by a personal contact with it, combined with the experiences related to me by unfortunate victims of the opium-smoking habit, as are those writers who have never invaded a "Chinatown" or have felt the "fellow-feeling" that kindles a glow of sympathetic warmth toward Ah Sin's unfortunate race.

That which I have beheld and heard lies with far more weight upon me, if possible, than the experiences through which I have passed with morphine, etc. And while I recognize that, in pleading the cause of others, I am but pleading my own, I yet feel immeasurably incompetent to do even meager justice to a subject so fraught with misery and despair to those infatuated with its seductive influence and never-relinquishing hold.

Large cities are as distinctively and geographically mapped into national or race sections as is the map of the world. For example, there is the Italian section, the Hebrew quarter, the African colony, the Irish constituencies, and the numerous other nationalities of the earth huddled together, but not yet sufficiently numerous to be designated by boundary lines. But Boston's "Chinatown" is uniquely distinctive from all the rest. The other "towns" swarm and bustle with noisy life, by men, women and children, and especially the latter, everywhere; but in Chinatown a woman is rare, and a child would be at a premium. The place is as quiet as they are noiseless. Even on Sunday, when the suburban cities and towns have augmented the Celestial quarter by the addition of hundreds, who come hither to get their Chinese luxuries, play "fan-tan" (the Chinaman's popular gambling game), smoke "opem," and go to Sunday school, they flit hither and thither, in a sort of Indian-file fashion, with their hands tucked away under their blouse-like garments, which gives to them a squab-shouldered appearance,— as noiselessly as denizens of the nether world. John is not a creature of mirth and hilarity, — that is, the opium-smoking John. He only laughs when under the transporting embrace of his demoniacal master — Opium. There is as much difference in the countenance of the Chinese Sunday school scholar, singing gospel songs, and his brother who prefers opium and "fan-tan," as there is between darkness and light, ir-

respective of his belief in Jesus or Confucius.   I account
for it in the genius of the spirit.   In my endeavor to find
the bottom of the opium-smoking habit, I studied it from
the standpoint of his professed Christianity.   I venture
to say it would be difficult to find gathered under one
church roof a body of professing followers of Christ who
could be found giving greater external evidences of being
"in the unity of the faith and the bonds of peace," than
was so strikingly made apparent in this truly brotherly
fellowship of a Chinese Sunday school.   But, again, it was
evident "that the harvest was great and the laborers few,"
for he was teacherless in the greater number of instances.
They were paragons of neatness and gentility, and together
with the uniformity of well-dressed heads, they presented
a unique picture.

The Chinaman may have the appearance and the manner of being "child-like and bland," but he is an accurate
observer and close student of human nature, and makes
few mistakes in "sizing up" the smart ones ; and in playing the part of innocent and simpleton, it is invariably
done to his financial gain and at the smart fellow's expense.

He is profoundly and almost invariably ignorant about
opium-smoking and opium "joints."   And I very much
doubt if a stranger, unfamiliar with the drug, would elicit
from a Chinaman an iota of reliable information in regard
to this momentous question.   I conversed with one who
told me that he was born in San Francisco ; and while I
found him familiar with gambling and the methods of his
more fortunate gaming "Christian " neighbor in obtaining
"protection," this genius in "the ways that are dark, and
tricks that are vain," professed absolute ignorance of the

existence of "joints" and the uses to which opium was put, and suspiciously stole away. Probably this accounts for the meager information obtainable by those not familiar with the habit. In this mystic opium circle there seems to exist a code of secrecy, yet its rites were never formulated into speech or uttered by human lips, but rather as the victim becomes confirmed in the vice, his whole nature seems swallowed up in cunning, duplicity and deception. He feels that he has upon him the mark of Cain, and the study of his life is in concealing his wretchedness and his identity from his associates. It is largely the same with gambling. Men sit side by side at the gaming-table, year in and year out, yet they will meet each other daily upon the busy thoroughfare, unknown and unrecognized, so far as visible outward signs go. Dante accurately describes a condition, however, where all the reserve barriers are thrown aside, and he becomes intensely earnest. Centuries of time has not changed the gambling spirit, no more than will the succeeding ones. He draws the picture in the spirit of one familiar with his theme, thus :—

> "When from their game of dice men separate,
> He who hath lost remains in sadness fixed,
> Revolving in his mind what luckless throws
> He cast; but, meanwhile, all the company
> Go with the other; one before him runs.
> And one behind his mantle twitches; one
> Fast by his side, bids him remember him.
> He stops not; and each one, to whom his hand
> Is stretched, well knows he bids him stand aside;
> And then he from the press defends himself."

So with opium's victims, so far as "giving it away" to the merely idly curious. Then, too, the Chinaman knows full well that it is one of the most potent weapons in the

hands of his enemy to his exclusion from American soil.
Hence, he is the embodiment of secretion on this evil.

  *   *   *   *   *   *

Confession may be good for the soul, but it is, to say
the least, very humiliating and embarrassing.   But to the
confessor are also made many confessions.   Hence arises
these thoughts on opium-smoking.   Speaking briefly from
a church platform, some months ago, on my morphine experience, at the close of the meeting, a young man, while
informing me that my delineation of opium's tortures were
accurate in those abandoning it, told me that he was a
victim of the "pipe-hitting" mania for it.   He said, in substance, that he hailed from New York; that for ten years
he had been practicing the vice; that he was an undone
and ruined man, and that to abandon its use was futile.
"Cures there are none that I will ever touch," he said,
"after the experience of a friend of mine just released
from an institution that makes a specialty of curing the
habit.   His people are wealthy, but the 'cure' broke him
up.   I prefer to stick to the 'pipe' rather than share my
friend's fate, and your experience shows no open door in
antidotes and a worse state in morphine."   In closing, he
said, "I am unable to work, and this habit has made of
me a thief!   This town is full of them!"

The pitcher that goes often to the well, sooner or later
meets with a catastrophe, and likewise is it with the thief.
He may run the gauntlet many a day, but like the cunning
fox, he will get careless and indifferent, and some day this
unfortunate young fellow will find himself in the meshes
of the law, and then there will come to him an experience
not unlike that of another misguided young man addicted

to the same curse. He frankly told me the sad circumstances of his having become enthralled, as an ignorant youth, in Quebec, to the use of opium, by a learned man of the clerical profession. He looked strong and well as he related to me the futile efforts he had made to break his prison bars of habit's growth. He now lies in the hospital of the Charlestown (Massachusetts) State Prison, where he has been confined for months for the transgression of this great physical law. I have heard the story of his alleged crime from the lips of his aged mother; and while her story makes her boy innocent, and a victim of circumstances,— a story that is probably true,— the opium smoking curse may safely be charged with the twenty years of imprisonment of himself and a female accomplice. I hope and trust that an unsolicited letter (portions of which will be appended to this chapter) which the author of these "Confessions" unexpectedly received from this unfortunate prisoner, may interest so deeply some philanthropic souls, that it may stir them to an investigation to ascertain whether or no these hastily tried and heavily sentenced prisoners have not been "more sinned against than sinning." But years or months, the unfortunate victim of opium can find no solace in prison. The Law, which locks within four walls by bolts and bars the felon, at the same turn of the key excludes the demons opium or rum, which dragged the hapless victims thither.

Another, after twelve years abandonment of "pipe hitting," wrecked and a periodical drunkard, told me that the legacy of frightful "creeping sensations" in his stomach only gave way to rum. His fifteen days without sleep and the agony he experienced "camosoled" in a hospital, leaves open no door of hope of relief again in the direction out of which he has come.   And so on *ad infinitum*.

"This town is full of them,"—opium-smokers, of course, — started a train of thought I could not well shake off. I felt satisfied that he told the truth, from the despairing manner in which he uttered the words.   The subject, however, has long since become a nauseating one to me, and the abundance of evidence obtainable from magazines, newspapers and individual experiences related have made it unnecessary to further demonstrate by a personal investigation the truth or falsity of his statements.   I finally concluded to "see" Boston's Chinatown at close range. What I saw and how I saw it, and what evidence I obtained of this peculiar habit and this peculiar people, may not be entirely void of interest.

*   *   *   *   *   *

But how is such evidence to be obtained from people so reticent as opium users, and so shrewd as Chinamen? is a question I propounded to myself.

" O, ask some one that is addicted to its use, and they will impart the needed knowledge," some one may say.

Finding a lost needle in a mow of hay, would be a comparatively easy undertaking in comparison with that of finding so "fresh" an individual as to plead guilty to such a heinous fault to so simple an interrogator.

" Well, then, ask a Christian Chinaman, or any one of them, for that matter, and he will be glad to tell you all about it," another wise one may suggest.

Go ask the wind from whence it came and whither it goeth, and the answer will be as clear and explicit as to its birth and destination, as will be the information of a reliable character that such a one would derive from so impertinent a question to a Chinaman on a slight acquaintance.

To go in company with one addicted to the vice or one made familiar with the haunts from an official capacity might be one way. A man's home, however, is his castle, whether he be prince or beggar, and no one has the right lawfully to cross the threshold of either uninvited.

"Seek and ye shall find ; knock, and it shall be opened unto you," is applicable to things material as well as spiritual, the law regulating them being observed.

The evidences of all things are about us, yet we perceive but very little of anything unless our minds are attracted to it, and we knock and search, and then a fathomless abyss of knowledge is opened before the vision, and we are made sensible of our finite condition, yet of our infinite possibilities. "I know a millionth part of one per cent about nothing," Edison, the great electrician, is reported to have said, expressive of the vastness of the possibilities of undiscovered power in electrical forces.

I visit a Chinese Sunday school, conversed with many, get an invitation to call on my Chinese "merchant" acquaintance, who has an eye to business, and is a shrewd and very intelligent "boy," as his tastefully written card demonstrates. Confession on my part opens the closed door, and I find that which I seek without deception. I talk opium from my standpoint of experience, and my friendly acquaintance promises to supply my "opem" wants in the shape of "pipe" and the drug whenever I choose to call.

    *   *   *   *   *   *

"Are you going to get your supper down there ?" asked

an acquaintance, who was conversant of my intention of visiting Chinatown. "There is a 'tony' restaurant down there if you get hungry. Nights it is frequented by the Harvard student and others in quest of 'life.'"

"No, I did not think of so doing," I replied. "I was not aware of the existence of such a place."

Years of experience about town had made me familiar with the fact that where "living pictures" were to be seen truest to Nature's plan, there the student, chaperoned by the experienced "fellah," was to be found, beholding and sipping in the nectar of death from the fountains of modern Babylon. And, no doubt, the revelations made by Rev. Parkhurst of New York to the "astonished" world, must have caused a smile of credulity as the panorama of "Boston inside out" passed before his mental vision; for the Harvard student has an open door to the hidden mysteries of vice, and "nothing new under the sun," or the moon's pale light, for that matter, long remains concealed from his ardent gaze. And this is not said in a derogatory spirit of the young man. He is largely a "country lambkin," with the same natural tendencies as other youth, but from his position, with time and money at his disposal, he is made a special target of by the archers of worldliness and vice. If knowledge can not be obtained from books wholly, experience makes up for the deficiency; and the worst wish the redeemed Opium Eater has for him is, that not a single soul among them might stray back to become victims of the vices upon which they feast.

*   *   *   *   *   *

On the upper landing of a dark staircase I saw the characters that informed me of the location of a Chinese restaurant. It was an uninviting looking place, as their domicils invariably are. I climbed the turning staircase, and at the landing, seeing and hearing no life, I tried and failed to open the door in the usual manner. I found that it had been arranged to slide into the wall, probably in order to economize space, for the Chinese have none to throw away. The door slid in with a bang, and two steps brought me at once into a dimly lighted room—the Celestials' dining room. But such a restaurant! In the small apartment, once the fashionable parlor of an old-time Bostonian, later on, in the neighborhood's swift decadence, the abode of the Camille, were now seated around two of the three large tables at least fourteen Chinamen, with chopsticks in hands, eating their frugal meal. At my intrusion they all suspended operations, and for a moment I surveyed the strange spectacle. As no one moved or spoke, I said, " Is this a restaurant? Can I get something to eat here?"

" No !" snarled out a Chinaman, at the farther table.

Not one of them resumed his eating.

" Not a cup of coffee ?" I asked.

" No coppee !" the same voice uncivilly yelled out.

" How about tea ?" I inquired.

" No tea, no nuttin," he replied, in his still ruffled voice.

" But," I said, " I was told I could get a supper here ; that you catered to the public—to Harvard students."

" Cross street," said a Celestial, near where I stood ; " cross street — thir-six."

And I felt thankful that this was not the place.

Across the street I went, expecting in my verdancy to find a very "swell " affair.

Standing in a doorway were two evil-looking specimens

of the Mongolian race. They were smoking their long pipes, and for all I know to the contrary might have been "covering" a fan-tan game or an opium joint.

"Where is that Chinese restaurant located?" I inquired.

"Upstairs," and he pointed to a dark, cut-throat looking entry and stairway.

The stairs climbed, the barely lighted room entered, and the "swell" Chinese restaurant of my fancy vanished, and the same scene greeted the eye — low, round tables, full of Chinamen, chop-sticks in hand, — except they were more numerous than in the place opposite. My intrusion "held them up" until all the questions and answers of the previous place had been gone through by one who acted as spoksman, and not less gruffly than his neighbor.

I studied the picture a little closer, which revealed that John is not particularly partial to adornments or a useless expenditure of money for what we are pleased to recognize as home comforts. Bare floors and walls are not attractive things to draw a refined and cultivated mind.

His whole mode of life denotes the sojourner and the transient. As I was not particularly interested in Chinatown from the epicurean standpoint, but rather the opium-smoking curse, I withdrew.

*   *   *   *   *   *

I consulted my card, and went to his place of business, which I will designate as a Chinese "merchant." His store consisted of the front parlor of a former dwelling-house, no alterations having taken place except, apparently, the putting in of a counter.

An infinite variety of Chinese goods, for the outer as well as the inner man, crowded the available space. Fish

and ducks, dried and smoked, that had the appearance of
having passed under a shovel factory trip-hammer, so bat-
tered out were they. There was an ugly looking bird's
leg, that had the appearance of sinews or dried-up strings
of meat wound about it, which Li informed me made a
"fine soup." [My opinion of Chinese "chicken" soup
will appear further on.]

As I entered Li's place, two young men who, if we may
be allowed to judge from appearances, might readily be
placed in the "tough" column of the city's denizens,
glanced up, and seeing me, one of them said to the Chinaman behind the counter, "I will be in tomorrow for that
tea," and they passed out. At which the really good looking and affable Sing Lee "smiled a smole" that was suggestive of "rats," as he said, "Y-e-s-s," and the opium-
smokers passed out.

This store seemed to be run on the co-operative plan,
five or six Chinamen being interested in the stock of goods.
I made a number of purchases, and found they possessed
the true Yankee spirit in trade, and knew a "freshy"
when they saw one. Why not? I never was entertained
better even at that. After a few calls, however, and we
got better acquainted, things were different.

While the co-operative plan was clearly manifest in this
harmonious shop, the number of sales of opium which were
made during my visits, including my own purchase, were
always made by a particular man. He was anything but
attractive in appearance, but agreeable enough on acquaintance. He was always on hand, however, felt-footed and
noiseless, as the unfortunate opium victim appears without
the counter, haggard and pale, and who without a word

lays before the dispenser of the drug "two bits," and a minute jar, so black with opium and dirt that its metal could not be named.   He was a little Chinaman, and had the appearance of having just awoke from his opium stupor.   I imagined that I detected the same look of contempt on the Chinese face at the unfortunate condition of his fellow-countryman, as that apparent in the manner and gesture of the trim-looking bartender in a fashionable drinking resort as he places the bottle of liquor before the dilapidated sot, whom some one has taken pity on and given a drink.

Pulling out a drawer, the Chinaman took from it a pair of old-fashioned balances, such as Justice holds in her uplifted hand.   He then turns a stick around in the tomato-like can of opium, and when a sufficient quantity of the dark, molasses-like mixture adheres to the stick he transfers about a large tablespoonful of it to the ink-black pot, weighs the precious elixir, and the buyer and the seller, as noiselessly as they came, without exchanging a word, depart.   This incident brought to mind the opium and morphine habit and my connection with it, and one of the objects of my visit being to get an opium-pipe and some of the drug, it opened up the way to ascertain the opinion of the Chinese on the opium habit.

"'Mopene,' no good. Very bad. China 'boy' smoke opium. China boy never use 'mopene,'" said one of the quartette, and he showed a perfect knowledge of its use by the reference that many women used morphine.

" Can the Chinese cure the opium habit?" I inquired of Sing, on one occasion, believing that the curse must have called for extended research among the medical men of China.

"Yer," Sing replied, and he smiled pleasantly as he caught my eye, and from out his wares he produced a small flat phial. It contained, perhaps, two dozen little black pills. He explained the manner of taking them,— a graduation process. They act as a temporary relief, and afford the suffering opium-smoker a short respite, as do many medicines in chronic disorders.

"But," he said, "they no cure 'opem' smoker; you nowee that."

"How much?" I asked, as the fabulous prices I had paid for morphine antidotes passed across my mind.

"Thirt' cents. No good!" and he threw it down.

And he sounded the market value and intrinsic worth of every opium, morphine and liquor cure medicine in the United States today, as a permanent, lasting remedy!

It was a genuine Chinese preparation, and, no doubt, like many for opium and liquor, had poisons of sufficient potency to temporarily benumb and paralyze the vital forces of life for quite a season.

*　　*　　*　　*　　*　　*

On one of my visits to the Chinese "merchant's" store I saw a sight that reassured me in my faltering determination to publish these "Confessions." It was that of a young man, perhaps four-and-twenty years of age. His face was smooth. Intelligence and refinement marked his well-shaped head, while his hands were those of one un-accustomed to manual toil. His dress was fashionable and tailor-made. His face was flushed, which heightened his exceedingly Prodigal cast of features. In his hand he carried an exquisitely carved box of Chinese workmanship and design, which was perhaps a foot long, by a few inches high and wide. An opium-smoker's 'kit,' I thought. He was smoking the nearest kin to the opium-pipe, in manner and also in deadly effect — a cigarette. The orb of light revealed that—

> "The image of a wicked, heinous fault
> Lives in his eye; that close aspect of his
> Doth show the mood of a much troubled breast."

Along with him appeared the opium dispenser. He did not use the balances in weighing out the twenty-five cents worth of the drug which the young man purchased, that he always did when the purchase was made by a Chinaman. Then, too, the Melican man did not get by a third what he gave his Chinese brother. The novel way in which he delivered the goods, interested me. He took an old playing-card,— perhaps it had done service for John in a desperate game, *a la* Bret Harte, but hardly likely, — and after running on it the opium daub, by a few movements he improvised out of it a neat little box.

"What's it?" asked Sing, smilingly.

"Seven spot of spades," replied the sober youth, and without comment went out.

If I were a necromancer, I would lament the significance of the card, and associating it with the deadly drug, together with his temperament, should say that spades would be triumphant over his life in seven cursed years.

Men in all ages of time have been fired by some incident trivial to the masses about them to right some great evil,—a Moses, a Christ, a John Brown, an Abraham Lincoln — in fact, the whole human race, when imbued by the Infinite Spirit. Rum and opium are the degradation of the human race! How are these foes to eternal happiness to be successfully fought unless the living God comes to the rescue and obliterate the lust for gain and power in an intelligence made perfect that all men are the objects of His watchcare, and that we cannot rise to mighty action unless infused by the fire divine? This youth stirred anew the flame to consecrate this work and my life to enlightening humanity, so far as in me lies, "that they come not into this torment!"

And when we behold the majestic effrontery whereby one man* has arisen and proclaimed himself the called and chosen instrumentality of "telling the truth" about the Bible, the Bible's Jehovah, Moses and the prophets, Christ and the apostles, surely the noble and God-loving among humanity ought to take heart and do mighty battle to save the generations yet unborn from debasing and vicious habits and leave their pathway in life strewn with literature which shall give them enlightenment and prevent them going down to death through ignorance of the infinite law, for the knowledge of which these same Bible characters made of this life living sacrifices of themselves by ignominious deaths!

*　　*　　*　　*　　*　　*

I made several visits to Li Hi Wong & Company's before I got my opium pipe. Li said that his stock was all gone, but that he would have some in a few days. Finally

---

*Somebody ought to tell the truth about the Bible. Ministers dare not do it; they would be driven from the pulpit. The presidents of the colleges and professors dare not do it, as they would lose their places; politicians dare not do it; they would be defeated. The editor dare not do it, for fear he would lose circulation. The rich man dare not do it, for fear he would lose caste. Merchants dare not do it, fearing they would lose trade; even a clerk dare not do it, for he would be discharged,— and so I thought I would do it myself. ["The Holy Bible," by Robert G. Ingersoll.

I secured one, and Li said the prices ranged from $2 to
$20. The Chinese, as every one knows, are inveterate
smokers of tobacco, and have a mania for gambling. The
long stemmed pipe, with its minute bowl, which is often
seen in their mouths as well as in their places of business, is not an opium-pipe, as almost everybody presumes.
It is a tobacco pipe. John's tobacco looks like Turkish.
It is heavy with nicotine. He puts a little into the pipe
and draws quick, and in a few minutes it is consumed. If
put into a large-bowl pipe with a short stem, the nicotine
would waste half of it, and the smoke would be uncomfortably hot in the mouth. Hence his pinch of the weed
and quick whiffs through the long, cooling stem. He is
very hospitable with his tobacco. It is in "common," and
they all help themselves from the same wooden bowl. I
have never seen a Chinaman filthy enough to chew tobacco.
He has a perfect detestation for alcoholic stimulation, and
the numerous barrooms about Chinatown contain no Celestial "bummers."

The following cut is a reproduction of the opium-smokers' pipe by the engraver's art, and is of a cheap quality :

This pipe is of bamboo, twenty-five inches long, and an
inch and a quarter in diamater. The ends are exactly as
the cut shows them, and are of bone or ivory, with no
mouth-piece whatever. The bowl is made of metal, and

Sing had glued it into the bamboo. A small carved piece of wood ornament, with Chinese characters, completed the outside of the pipe. At the bottom of the bowl is a "rest" upon which the "cooked" opium pill is placed.

In preparing opium for smoking, the Chinese extract all that water will dissolve, and then evaporate to dryness, under a process which they call "cooking," and make it into little pills. One of these they put into the pipe, inhale a few puffs at a time, or one single, long puff, and return the smoke through the nostrils. This they repeat until the necessary dose has been taken. The relationship existing between the opium-smoking Chinaman and the cigarette habitué is so close as not to need comment.

And, while my Chinamen friends furnished me with pipe and "two bits'" worth of opium — and a *bit* it was, too, which he poured into the half of a Chinese nutshell, —they would not "load" the pipe ready for "hitting" for me. I was glad, indeed, of this, for in it I recognized the birthmark of God, and appreciated their warning to me never to "hit the pipe."

"Come with me, some day, I show you all about it ; but you no smoke," said the evil-looking dispenser, now grown kindlier looking, as he shook my hand at parting.

Better gaze upon the upturned faces of the ghastly dead in the great city's morgue, than look upon the living spectacles of an opium "joint."

To what extent Chinamen are victims of the opium-smoking habit can best be told by those who live continuously among them. I should say that it is as universal as the drink habit among Americans.

"The mills of the gods grind slow, but they grind exceeding small," and the opium-smoking victims throughout Christendom are but receiving the receding wave of the opium curse which the English-speaking race forced upon China.

Unless I have been misinformed, druggists do not deal in this peculiar preparation of opium. Hence, the victims of this form of vice primarily receive their instruction from the Chinese. I am informed, however, that in large cities opium joints are conducted by others than Chinamen.

* * * * * *

It approaches the midnight hour. Chinatown has an almost deserted aspect from an outward view. Standing on the spot made historical by forty years of residence by Wendell Phillips, I read from a marble tablet these words, " Here Wendell Phillips resided for forty years, devoted by him to efforts to secure the abolition of American slavery in this country. The charms of home, the enjoyment of wealth and learning, even the kindly recognition of his fellow-citizens were by him accounted as naught, compared with duty. He lived to see justice triumphant, freedom universal, and to receive the tardy praise of his former opponents. The blessings of the poor, the friendless, and the oppressed enriched him. In Boston he was born, November 29, 1811, and died February 2, 1884. This tablet was erected in 1894, by order of the City Council of Boston."

From this view I study the surrounding picture. Cold blasts of penetrating air and clouds of dust sweep down the avenue. Out from the dimly lighted abodes of the Celestials an occasional Chinaman emerges. He evidently does not relish the cold, raw November wind. After

looking in all directions, he suddenly seems to gather himself together, as the ladies do their skirts when about to
cross a muddy thoroughfare (only John seems to have suspended his from his shoulders), and hies himself across
the street at a Chinaman's trot, regardless of crosswalks,
and disappears into a basement or dark alley.   John is not
a street-corner loafer.   He has too much to attend to for
that.   Within, as you pass along, groups ranging from four
to eight or ten, sit in close proximity to the stove, nearly
all of them with their long tobacco pipes in hand or in
their mouths.   The scene is as primitive as that of the
country tavern or the village store in New England rural
life, where farmers gather of an evening and talk "crops"
and "hoss." It would be interesting to know what themes
occupy their attention.   I walk around through the quarter,
and quiet reigns supreme.   Their quaint, flaring business
signs, in Chinese characters, are striking.   "Free Masons
up stairs," together with Chinese characters, placarded
above an open door, which revealed an entry and front
room liberally strewn with large dry goods boxes, was one
of their peculiar signs.   There is not much doubt, however,
but that something mystic and mysterious was hidden
beneath the mere words, and that to the initiated it meant
fan-tan, or an opium joint, perhaps.

The sharp night air chills me, and I retire to Brigham's
well-known restaurant, where a Rip Van Winkle might
have entered after a twenty odd years' sleep and not have
noted scarcely a single change.   The retinue of colored
waiters are there, and the same routine of business goes
on as it did long years ago, before the writer's day.   The
courteous waiter brings me a pewter pot of coffee, which,

diluted to the extreme of weakness, warms me up and affords me a powerful stimulant, even though I am now a "dissipated," yet redeemed Opium Eater. I realized as great a transition in my temporary renewal of "old ways," as Rip found in the changed condition of things in the village of the Catskills, as related by Washington Irving.

But the restaurant. The "fad" of Chinatown. And, like all fads, it was a financial success. It was one of the two previously described. The dark and gloomy setting of round tables, Chinamen and chopsticks, had, like an act from a play on the mimic stage by the mechanic's art, undergone a transformation, and a brilliantly lighted scene had taken their place.

I follow a half dozen beardless youths up the stairs. Business was not booming, but a thriving trade was going on. The round tables in the center of the floor had given place to unique looking ones. They were higher by several inches than ordinary tables, and the low wooden benches upon which the patrons sat at the tables, looked very antiquated indeed. However, they served a good purpose. The revellers, often more or less inebriated, did not have far to carry their food, and they were also convenient to rest their drooping elbows on without much exertion. Ranged about the sides of the room, within reach, were small, heavy projections for tables, with the same heavy and stupid-looking benches, adapted for two persons. There was no attempt at concealment, by the use of curtained slips, or screens, and everything was exposed to view. The tables were as devoid of eating-house utensils as are the tables, on Sunday, of a first-class liquor saloon with a victuallers' license.

Young fellows, of "seedy" appearance, were eating a soup at thirty cents a bowl, without bread and butter or a single accompaniment, and which, if served gratutiously under other circumstances, would have been repudiated. It would have produced a riot in any penal institution in the land, and Oliver Twist would never have gained fame by asking for a second serving of it. Such, however, is a " fad."

Seated at one of the miniature side tables, where I could command a good view of my "fadist " revelers, I noted in my dreamy way my companions. At my elbow, so closely that we touched, sat a young woman with her male escort. He was the perfection of style, and could have rendered valuable service as a model for a fashion plate, with his full beard and English cast of features. They were both smoking the deadly cigarette. Between rests of their peculiar Chinese viands, she blew clouds of the noisome smoke into her companion's face. If I may be pardoned for using the noble horse as descriptive of fallen woman, she was a good feeder, but evidently not cheaply kept. She had good points, was smooth, and very fast. Had nature been allowed her kindly sway, uninterrupted by vice's domination, she would have been stouter and coarser looking ; but in her dissipated career and unholy life she was "refined" after the manner produced by the no less pernicious practice of her sex in their use of cosmetics or powerful poisons to beautify their complexions. The only expression I heard from her, as they made their exit, was the remark "that she heard the clock strike three and four that morning."

Across the small room a sister of shame, on the road to

ruin, was making equally as good time to break life's
record as my neighbor, and if looks were any criterion
she had the "pole" in this swift race for death.   As she
passed out, enveloped in a cloud of smoke from her cigar-
ctte, I saw her give a smile of recognition to the woman
near me ; and, as the smoke ascended from her once pure
lips, there was revealed a handsome but hopeless face.

Others, similarly engaged, occupied postions about the
room.   The clean, intelligent-looking China "boy," with a
far-away look, asked for my order.

"What have you ?" I asked, there being no bill-of-fare.

"Chicken soup," he answered.

"Is that all the variety of soups you have ?" I asked.

"That 's all," he replied.

I ordered it.   In a few moments he brought me an ordinary Yankee tin coffeepot, holding nearly a quart, full
of hot tea, with a small, cheap cup.   There were neither
milk, sugar or spoon.   The half hour wait before he
served the "soup," showed a degree of wisdom in this
manner of waiting.   Alcoholic stimulation being more or
less indulged in among the patrons, the soothing influence
of hot tea might in a measure counteract the liquor's fumes.

There were no loitering Chinamen about the place.

There was nothing "soupy" looking about the soup —
no rich, oily surface,— and the dark, watery looking fluid,
steaming like boiling water, was suggestive of anything
but soup.   The plated spoon and a tiny little dish, which
contained a liquid of a dark-reddish color, a relish for the
ingredients before me, completed the frugal order, at fam-
ine rates.   I sipped it.   It was tasteless and flat.   A little
of the relish gave it a stimulating flavor, and I threw it

all in. I took courage and felt for the bottom — for the
chicken. I brought up a spoonful of a substance of a
stringy nature, odorless, that brought vividly to mind a
lot of bleached-out angleworms, and with the persistency
of a desperate deed, I flavored them. The crushing process was reminiscent of boyhood days, when I recalled
the potato patch and my grandsire mashing potato bugs.
Such is prejudice and a lack of the epicurean's talent. I
saw no one else who seemed to be dissatisfied. In eating
and drinking I am a law unto myself. I would not dis-
parage Chinese cooking and victuals on so short an acquaintance, but good old New England dishes will ever re-
tain a hallowed place in my heart against the conglomerate
masses of food that I saw being indulged in about me, and
which was provocative of restlessness, as was suggested
by my cigarette-smoking sister, who unwillingly had listened to the clock's early peal.

There was no boisterous noise of drunken revelry here.
The curious or satisfied ones passed out, and others took
their places. Two of Boston's "finest" entered, and the
door of the grated "cage," behind which the cashier sat,
admitted them to his presence. They passed through the
place, and the significance of law and government was
wonderfully made apparent in their uniformed presence as
they silently passed out.

The women frequenters, seen under other conditions,
would not have attracted special note. They were American, and more than ordinarily good-looking. Two women
with a single male escort, dressed in rich material and with
sealskin garments, and who would readily have commanded
a prominent sitting in the fashionable congregations of

worship on the Lord's Day, had driven down to take their
midnight lunch from food prepared by Celestial hands,
instead of patronizing the fashionable café.   Their jeweled
hands betrayed their unholy life.   They dealt in a bondage more cursed and far-reaching than African slavery!

There passed out two young women, whose unsteady
gait drew my gaze.   Their attire denoted tastefulness, but
the ashy, ghost-like whiteness of their faces, and their general demeanor, brought vividly before me my own ghastly
countenance under my first opium experience.   The flush
of alcoholic stimulation was wanting; that of narcotic
imbibition was plainly manifest.   A youth, after his first
attempt with a quid of tobacco or his first pipe or cigar,
never presented a more sickening spectacle.   The aged
Chinese waiter smiled as approvingly upon them, as he assisted them to the door, as one might imagine in the look
of delight on the face of the betrayer of man's first mother!

The scenes merely called to mind the same vices made
familiar in the redeemed Opium Eater's life twenty odd
years ago, but in a different form.   The business was conducted as legitimately and open as any first-class establishment.   As an American enterprise, it would fail before it started.   It could not exist without rum, and the
exorbitant rates for food, and its openness, would not be
conducive as an attraction, when seclusion and abandonment can be had for a trifling pittance.

Hence, the Chinese restaurant "fad" is a great financial
success, for which, no doubt, Hong Far Low & Co. have
to contribute a goodly sum to the powers that rule for the
"special dispensation" of being all-night venders of their
peculiar viands to dissipated "fadists."

As I passed into this rum-plagued district, the results of the undemocratic principle of making a "privileged" class of the licensed saloon keepers were visible in the drunken specimens of youthful manhood and womanhood, and the filthy language that assailed the ear from these short-lived transgressors.

To be just, all men should receive an equitable recompense for their deeds, good or bad. I trust that in the cycles of eternity the grantors of this unholy indulgence will never be compelled to remain in chains longer than a time sufficient to have burned into their souls impressions everlasting, that it is not profitable to traffic in a substance which causes multitudes of defenseless women and children to live lives that are a curse by day and a terror by night, and that is not matched by Dante's inferno. Rather let us have free barrooms than "licensed" saloons; but better still, let there be no places where can be bought commodities for the destruction of mankind.

*   *   *   *   *   *

As I lay upon my sleepless couch, the active brain and restless eye refuse the weary body's pleading behest to retire to dreamland. Either the coffee or the "soup," or both, had produced insomnia, and in quick and repeating succession the scenes of the night, panorama-like, passed in review, while the clock's measured striking of the early morning hours, brought my erring sister in folly forcibly to mind. Out of the silence so hushed and still, a voice so clear and sweet that I would with reluctance exchange it for a seraph's, called,—

" P-a-r-p-a !" A short pause—and " P-a-r-p-a."

"What, dear?" I answered to the summons.

"Ain't you glad tomorrow is Thanksgiving?" my only child, six years old, asked.

"Why, my child?" (I am an interrogation point with my little one.)

"So you won't have to go to work, and you can lay in bed till nine o'clock," replied my little daughter.

And as I turned over the precious bundle of flannel, sweetness, and immortality, I devoutly thanked God that the crooked had been made straight, and that a spirit as solicitious for the well-being of your child as for my own had come into my once dark life; and, above all, the hope that these little ones may be wisely instructed to meet life's issues, armed with that invincible of armors—virtue.

*   *   *   *   *   *

From a recent newspaper clipping I give the lesson which John Burns, M. P., the noted English labor leader, gathered from a hasty visit to New York's Chinatown, and what he beheld in the early morning hours. He had as an escort one of Gotham's policemen. Mr. Burns saw:—

"The Chinese smoking opium in their own rooms, which is, however, perfectly legal, so long as it is not sold there. The policeman maintained that there was not an opium den in Chinatown. They were leaving a Chinese restaurant in Mott street, when a party entered which caused Mr. Burns to open his eyes wide with astonishment. Led by a Chinaman and two young white toughs, were two women, rather good looking, and a young girl, who seemed to be not more than fifteen years of age, but of a type rather common in Chinatown.

" 'Well, we wouldn't allow that in London,' Burns said. 'Just think of it! Such places open at two o'clock in the morning, and young men and women allowed to go there, regardless of whether they are married are not!' "

The following extracts I take from Dr. Keeley's pamphlet, "The Morphine User," and leave it with his vast experience as an earnest of the truthfulness of the description :—

The contrast between the whispered hush of an opium den or "joint," with its pungent, acrid odors, and its prostrate, silent human forms, and the hurrying rush and roar of traffic along the street without, is very great and very suggestive. The existence of the confirmed opium-smoker becomes as widely separated and apart from the active life of men, as the place of his resort is unlike the noisy thoroughfare and the busy marts of trade. In the end — an end certain and unescapable in its steady approach — the opium-smoker — he who tempts the " Sorcery of Madjoon "— drops out of real life, and passes his few remaining days in a world made up of the falsest unrealities and dreams. The opium or morphine user can mingle with his fellow-men; he has no need to go to some prepared place, and remain there for hours to experience the effects of his opiates; but the opium-smoker must devote time to burning the pungent incense with which he compels the inspiration of his god, and can only do this in a temple fitly prepared for this Satanic worship.

The ordinary pulverized and dry opium found in drug stores is not capable of producing the intoxicating effects in which opium-smokers revel. Several of my patients report having tried it, either alone or mixed with tobacco, but failed entirely to produce any opiumization. The drug must go through a special process in order to prepare it for effective smoking. As imported for use in opium dens it is quite unlike the crude gum of commerce, having been subjected to repeated washings, and has a dark, thick syrup or tar-like appearance and consistency. A little of this substance is held upon a wire in the flame of a small lamp, where it boils or becomes "cooked." It is then daubed upon the bowl of a pipe, specially prepared for the purpose, an opening is made through it to secure draft, and then the smoker turns the pipe-bowl to the flame, inhales three or four whiffs of smoke, and the "pipe" is exhausted.   A few quick expirations of smoke are called a "short draw," which is varied by a long, steady inhalation followed by the expulsion of the smoke through the nostrils.   This latter is called the "long draw."   This process is repeated again and again, beginners being satisfied with a half drachm weight of the drug, or even less, while habitués and confirmed opium-smokers, and Americans at that, have been known to consume three ounces at a single visit to their "den."   In these dens, then, the dissipated souls of humanity have "surcease from sorrow," and the exactions of weary life.   In these dens is the worship of the multiple god, "Madjoon," carried on every hour in the twenty-four.   Votaries from the best and worst walks of life worship at this shrine.   Time and money count for nothing.   Life itself, thrown in the balance, counts not a featherweight.   Friends, family, ambition, everything that makes life sweet, is lost to them while they burn the pungent incense.

The number of Americans who indulge in opium-smoking is constantly increasing.   Recent investigations of the subject lately made reveal this fact, and show that the victims of the habit are to be found in "good society," as well as among those living in the shadowed half of the world.   Richly dressed ladies coming from costly residences upon the avenues can be seen alighting from carriages and going down into the subterranean opium joints in New York and other large cities.   It is said that those who are able to have, and even do have, all the outfit for opium-smoking at their homes, prefer to smoke in some opium haunt.   So-called "respectable" ladies, and actresses of note, may be found mingled with outcasts of their own, and with all classes of the other sex, in this unlively, silent fellowship.   There is no noise of revelry; all dangerous passions are dulled and absorbed in the one overmastering appetite for the narcotic intoxication. The expenditure of money for the costly gratification drains the purse of the victim, and the time required, which is taken from active thought and life, causes neglect of business and social duties, while the heights of exhilaration are speedily and necessarily succeeded by reactive effect upon the nervous system. Thus in business and social life, in body and mind, the opium-smoker grows rapidly weak and worthless. He hastens toward an end of appalling horror — the period when every nerve and artery and vein, every muscle and every sinew in his body, will cry and shriek for their accustomed sedative, while it can no longer quiet them. The drug loses its power ; the system has been fed to the full of opium, the nerves have felt the last possible thrill of narcotic exhilaration, and the day of agony and death has dawned !

George Parsons Lathrop, in an article on opium-smoking which appeared some years ago in Scribner's Monthly, giving a description of a New York opium joint patronized by the lowest class of Chinese, says :—

"At the back of the room is an opening into another blind apartment, where we dimly make out certain bunks placed one over the other around the walls, for the convenience of confirmed and thoroughly stupefied opium debauchees. From one of these a lean, wan face, belonging to a creature who is just arousing himself from his long drugged sleep, stares out upon us with terrible eyes—eyes that dilate with some strange interior light ; ferocious yet unaggressive eyes ; fixed full upon us, and yet absolutely devoid of that unconscious response for which we look in human eyes as distinguishing them from those of brutes. This is the gaze of what is called an 'opium devil'—one who is supremely possessed by the power of the deadly narcotic on which he has leaned so long. Without opium he cannot live ; though human blood runs in his veins, it is little better than poppy juice ; he is no longer really a man, but a malignant essence in forming a cadaverous human shape."

"And even this stage is not the last ; there is a depth below this deep, when the poison has done all its work — when the corrupted currents of the blood no longer vitalize the system ; then the end comes ! It is an end to which many intelligent Americans, as well as multitudes of degraded Chinamen, are hastening, and in the case of those as well as these, the end is horror, despair and death !" [Dr. Leslie E. Keeley's "The Morphine User."

Dr. Medhurst, in describing the opium-smoker of China, says : "The outward appearances are sallowness of the complexion, bloodless cheeks and lips, sunken eye, with a dark circle round the eyelids, and a haggard countenance. There is a peculiar appearance of the face of a smoker not noticed in any other condition ; the skin assumes a pale, waxy appearance, as if all the fat were removed from beneath the skin. The hollows of the countenance, the eyelids, fissure and corners of the lips, depression at the angle of the jaw, and the temples, take on a peculiar dark appearance ; not that resulting from chronic diseases, but as if some dark matter were deposited beneath the skin. In fine, a confirmed opium-smoker presents a most melancholy appearance, haggard, dejected, with a lack-lustre eye and a slovenly and feeble gait." [North American Review.

Dr. Ball draws the following picture as the result of opium-smoking in the Flowery Kingdom : "Throughout the districts of China may be seen walking skeletons,— families wretched and beggared by drugged fathers and husbands,— multitudes who have lost house and home, dying in the streets, in the fields, on the banks of the river, without even a stranger to care for them while alive and, when dead, left exposed to view till they become offensive masses."

The saloons of America furnish a counter picture to that produced by the Chinese opium "joints," in the same wrecked specimens of humanity walking about as tramps and vagabonds, and also in the desolated firesides and cursed offspring.

* * * * * *

THE HYDRATE OF CHLORAL.

The redeemed Opium Eater having had quite an extensive experience with the hydrate of chloral previous to his morphine taking, and as its use and abuse is alarmingly prevalent, he incorporates herewith the opinions of those best suited to affirm whereof they speak. Dr. B. W. Richardson, of London, England, who by his early experiments did much to call the attention of the medical profession to chloral, and to encourage its use, expressed regret, later, that he had been instrumental in introducing a drug so capable of abuse, and which when abused wrought such disastrous results. He says in part :—

" It is a matter of deep regret that since the name has been given to the habit, Chloralism has become widespread. . . . Among the men of the middle class, among the most active of these in all its divisions — commercial, literary, medical, philosophical, artistic, clerical— Chloralism, varying in intensity of evil, has appeared. In every one of these classes I have named, and in some others, I have seen the sufferers from it, and have heard their testimony in relation to its effects upon their organizations,— effects exceedingly uniform, and, as a rule, exceedingly baleful. . . . Those people who come into the state of sleeplessness through excessive alcoholic stimulation, at first wake many times in the night with coldness of the lower limbs, cold sweatings, startings and restless dreamings. In a little time they become nervous about submitting themselves to sleep, and before long habituate themselves to watchfulness and restlessness, until a confirmed insomania is the result. Worn out with sleeplessness, and failing to find any relief that is satisfactory or safe in their false friend, Alcohol, they turn to Chloral, and in it find, for a season, the oblivion which they desire, and which they call rest. It is a kind of rest, and is, no doubt, better than no rest at all; but it leads to the unhealthy state that we are now conversant with, and it rather promotes than destroys the craving for alcohol. In short, the man who takes to chloral after alcohol, enlists two cravings for a single craving, and is doubly shattered in the worst sense."

Dr. Keeley says of chloral : "So potent an agent, one able almost, as with a blow, to produce concussion of the brain, to stupefy the patient, must of necessity be a dangerous one, or at least probably dangerous. . . . The evidence is overwhelming that in at least a considerable portion of the cases the continuous use of chloral hydrate establishes a habit, and one which is often more rapidly destructive than the opium habit. . . . The habitual use of chloral often occasions acute pains in the lower limbs, and often the patient becomes unable to use the legs. Vertigo, and partial and even complete paralysis, have resulted from the same cause. . . . In frogs, to which a fatal dose of chloral had been given, the whole heart was gorged with blood, having suffered complete paralysis. Palpitation of the heart, and irregular action of that organ, are frequent accompaniments of the habit. Chloral disorganizes the blood, causing eruptions, bleeding from the mucous membranes, falling off of the hair, and anæmia and dropsy. Not infrequently a dose no larger than those habitually taken will cause death. In cases less immediately fatal, the victim becomes a physical wreck, his mind becomes childish, and he soon dies."

*   *   *   *   *   *

The redeemed Opium Eater feels constrained in closing this work to engraft into it a few of the thoughts and suggestions found in Dr. Keeley's more recent publication, "Opium : Its Use, Abuse, and Cure." Enough has been gathered, I trust, in these pages to show the reader the only "cure" I can *knowingly* vouch for. However, my literary creed being eclectic, I most heartily indorse the sentiments found in them. And while laws are absolutely necessary, we are vastly more in need of men with sufficient character to execute righteously those laws already in existence, than a multiplicity of new ones. Hence, he who is wise will need no rod, and the fool will find no balm for this curse in "cures." He says in part : —

Every year our Legislatures are called upon to enact laws on a multiplicity of subjects affecting the general welfare of the people. It is surprising amongst the many reforms proposed, some attention has not been given to the traffic in opium. It is true that strenuous efforts have been made to prohibit the manufacture and sale of ardent spirits in some States, with partial success; but even the advocates of Temperance do not yet seem to have apprehended the magnitude and enormity of the opium habit and its consequence to the nation. This may be accounted for, to some extent, by the widespread ignorance prevalent concerning this subject.

The foregoing pages portray the nature of the Opium habit in all its details; they give careful statistics of its

growth and extent, and show the results of this unholy
traffic.   If it increases in the next twenty-five years in the
same proportion in which it has during the last quarter of
the century, it will be the greatest curse of the age !   And
there is no reason to suppose that the increase will be in
any smaller proportion, judging from the statistics of the
last ten years and the present and prospective condition
of the American people.

When we fully realize the awful consequences of this
traffic upon human life, domestic relations, and commercial
interests, it is something appalling to contemplate.   We
are accustomed to look with horror on the slaves of alcohol
in all their wretched degradation, and we seek to suppress
the trade in alcoholic liquors, and to reform the drunkards
of our community.   But if we could see the inner life of
at least a million and a half of our people, we should find
that they are slaves to a worse enemy than Alcohol, bound
in fetters compared with which those of alcohol are but
bands of straw; and who are being pitilessly dragged
down the steep and dismal path to death.   They are the
slaves of Opium and Morphine !

When this is generally understood and appreciated (and
I trust this book will have its influence in this direction
upon the minds of the people), there is no doubt but that
a popular outcry will be raised against a traffic so detri-
mental to health, happiness, and life, and fraught with
such danger to the nation.   .   .   .   Our public schools
ought to teach plain, primary truths, at least, concerning
the nature and danger of opium.   We have met with hundreds of adults in the past year, many of them energetic
business men, who never saw any opium or morphine to
know it, and who never knew of a single case of opium
using.   It is not right to allow children to grow up in profound ignorance of the nature and effect of a drug which
is commonly used amongst us, and which is so destructive
to all who use it.   If people were more thoroughly acquainted with it, it would be more generally avoided; but

while the great masses are ignorant concerning it, and it is freely prescribed by doctors and dispensed by druggists, we must expect a large and continued increase of the victims of the opium and-morphine habit.

There should be State legislation as to the sale of morphine and opium. A State board of health should be empowered to suppress patent medicines containing opium in any form (this would do away with most of the "opium antidotes" now on the market), and punish its venders. . . During the last few years they have been springing up like sudden fungus growth all over the land, sending their useless, or even poisonous, mixtures to thousands of the victims of opium, and collecting from them sums which, in the aggregate, reach almost incredible figures.

And what Dr. Keeley says in regard to others, may in truth apply to his own opium "cure." When the earnest and honest reformers understand the multiplication table of exhilarations and stimulations as put into operation by the subcutaneous injections of ANY poisons, and also the injurious after effects arising therefrom, they may hesitate before endorsing that of which they have no knowledge. Time will demonstrate the efficacy of rum and opium "cures," and the redeemed Opium Eater hazards no prophecy when he predicts that "the law of the Lord," which is perfect, and which deals with life even before its conception in the womb, and the enlightened intelligence, which must accompany its observance, is alone the panacea of *all* the ills from which the world is suffering.

God is Love. He also is Law!

www.ingramcontent.com/pod-product-compliance
Lightning Source LLC
Chambersburg PA
CBHW020354030726
47496CB00007B/2128